ENSEMBLE

8th House Publishing
Montreal, Canada

Copyright © 8th House Publishing 2015

First Edition

All rights reserved under International and Pan-American Copyright Conventions. No part of this book may be reproduced in any form or by any electronic or mechanical means, including information storage and retrieval systems, without permission in writing from the publisher, except by a reviewer, who may quote brief passages in a review.

Published in Canada by 8th House Publishing.
Front Cover Artwork by 8th House Publishing

Designed by 8th House Publishing.
www.8thHousePublishing.com

Set in Adobe Caslon Pro, BorisBlackBoxx and Rough Typewriter.

Library and Archives Canada Cataloguing in Publication

Phillips, Thomas, 1969-, author
    Ensemble / by Thomas Phillips. -- First edition.

ISBN 978-1-926716-29-9 (pbk.)

    I. Title.

PS3616.H57E57 2014   813'.6   C2014-904384-8

ENSEMBLE

by

Thomas Phillips

One

I CATCH HIM ON HIS BACK, drifting in thought beneath the window. What's the soundtrack? *Erik Satie. A Gnossienne, yes, No. 5.* Light entering through the half-open blinds in a to and fro. Clichés, readily admitted. But the light has a promising, stately grandeur, much like the music. And why shouldn't he spend his time this way? He, a small part of what theologians call very generally the Flesh, my husband, drifting in thought, or perhaps remaining static there, concentrating on some matter known only to him. This is how I find him, a common practice. It's how he is, my husband, Maurice, an accomplished professional, well-respected, well-liked, beneath the window in a state of floor-level reflection. But something is lacking in the recesses of his solitary, moving thought, or in the stasis that grips hold of the mind. And this absence, I am certain, is what guides his otherwise gentle reveries.

Best not to presume that the relative busyness of one's day-to-day is more important than the contemplation that unfolds in this light, on a mid-afternoon such as this, lying on the floor. He's doing the best he can. This use of time is important to him, to his work and his personal life, which are at a very profound level one and the same. Best to withhold your judgment. Don't dismiss his contemplation, his apparent inadequacy. My suspicions, my distrust, these are my problem.

But perhaps such counsel gets me off on the wrong foot. A foot stricken by plantar fasciitis. That terrible inflammatory condition whereby connective tissues of the appendage are undermined, let's say, to a point of debilitation, making it difficult to bend toes, land on the heel, walk, much less run. It's common to runners. I'm a runner. I wish we all were. Obesity, stroke, bone and muscle loss, cancer, depression, each operating at all-time highs in this epoch of mental busyness and sedentary lifestyles. Running helps; it prevents. But it's my fault, really, starting out like this, not unlike an athletic injury. I've been nervous, edgy, of late. I don't know what he's thinking, there on the floor, or anywhere, and it unhinges me. My chest has been sore.

Of course, I do know what he's thinking. In retrospect. I'm not an imbecile. I've spoken to her, in fact; to the object of his contemplation. She told me everything she knew. Very little about herself, as it happens. And he's already gone, departed, without necessarily having died. He left a note explaining it all in great detail, my husband. He's a philosopher by trade, after all. So I'm jumping back in time a bit (this is inevitable, and really, what is time? Maurice likes to ponder this question), to his place on the floor beneath the window, where he can think only of her.

I barely exist in such moments. Nothing is alive to him outside his thoughts of her there, or anywhere he happens to be really. Impossible to think of him at the head of the class, teaching under these circumstances, but taught he did (everyone loves him—almost everyone—he's a force of clear, directed thought in the classroom), until he disappeared. Now I'm alone with my own thoughts, memories. Reflections on what it was to be a wife in the presence of her husband over dinner, shared experiences; on how I came to be driven away from the space of his introspection and what this means to me now.

Monday. A new week. I catch him alone at his desk at home, he's talking to himself. This happens sometimes. To the point of it feeling a little dodgy, a little unsafe. Another professor, once a notable man, now lives on the streets here and carries on such discussions with himself. One can't help but run into him on occasion and be reminded of our mutual fallibility. I also talk to myself sometimes. Don't we all. A sad state of affairs, to be so deluded, disenfranchised of his sanity, this former professor, especially when that sanity was once so refined. He wanders the city pushing all he owns in garbage bags tied to a broken bicycle. His clothes are grubby, his hair unbridled, he stinks of accumulated perspiration. But this condition can also overtake the amorous subject. Especially when the object of desire is always one among many (thirty, to be exact), irretrievably distant in the classroom and hidden in her personal ethos; when circumstances preclude my beloved husband speaking to her directly among the other students, so that he needs to carry on these monologues with himself, with her. Maurice converses with her when she's not around. I know this about him. She has no idea. Or perhaps she does. Maybe on some level she intuits his communication from another part of the city. I prefer not to venture too deep into questions of temporal-spatial collapse. The fact of the matter is that Maurice talks to himself and only becomes aware of this oddity when I catch him. He smiles; he has a lovely smile, still youthful, and speaks of some idea or other, some benign preoccupation when I confront him. On this day he mutters some hazy comment about May of 68, student revolts in Paris, philosophers throwing bricks. Now he throws love-heavy bricks through the once solid windows of his mental acuity. It took too long for me to understand. I should have been more perceptive, though it wouldn't have made a difference in the face of his mounting desire. Her face, I've come to realize, her student face, is in fact uncommonly stirring.

Now I'm alone, another teacher, like him, abandoned but for my own students, colleagues. It's tremendously difficult to make a living as a musician and composer. One teaches, at first, with the idea that a position with an orchestra will emerge, or a star recording. But no, not for me. And really, who wants to play with an orchestra? It's mechanical, it glazes over one's being. Or so my orchestra friends tell me. They don't have the leisure to think about music outside the canon. I have ample time for this. I sit at my piano and play. On a good day, the light through the windows illuminates my playing; it shifts the tempo of being. I don't wish to philosophize, that's his territory. But the light strikes the keys in concert with my fingers. It opens into the room; sound and light, music and color conjoin to beget a place of solace. I am more myself there, at the piano, than at any other moment. When clouds darken the space, intervene in the light, for it is still light, I invariably play something melancholic. I succumb to the direction, the conducting we might say, of weather.

My colleagues are more or less in the same position. We continue to teach, but really, who doesn't want to play with an orchestra? There are limitations, to be sure. A pompous man waving a stick, conducting with his arrogance. I studied under such a man. Had I studied with a finer specimen of the human race, perhaps I would be performing with an orchestra after all, making my living with Brahms, Shostakovich, Britten…. The list is long and severe. Though I can't speak for my colleagues. They have their own stories, their own limitations with which to contend. What they don't have is my husband and his struggle to abandon us in the dust of an indefatigable desire.

I catch him on his back beneath the window. The window is open and a breeze compels the blinds to sway. Light dances in clear little movements, lands on his thoughts as he labors to focus, or extinguish them.

I lie beside him for a moment before I leave. I turn his head to face me. One of his hairs, a single hair, blows up and down over my nose with every breath—all of this lively movement comprising an otherwise still morning. I ask him if he loves me and he tells me he does. 'I went through your purse to find some cream,' he says next, 'and then again, later, when I still couldn't find any. Why are you carrying an exceedingly large pair of scissors in your purse?' he asks.

'To cut something,' I say.

Even he must admit, if only to himself, that

this abbreviated response warrants thought over and against whatever has been occupying him of late.

We are all, the three of us, more or less in our thirties. More for him, actually, but why become bogged down by numbers. His is a sensibility that retains many vestiges of youth. His body, too, belies his age. Until recently. Until he began to drift from me, from the regular circuits of his life. The stereotype of the philosopher who shrinks into the labyrinthine passages of the mind, neglecting the body while it grows to horrific proportions to resemble awkwardly shaped fruit—this is not Maurice. No, not until she burrowed into his thoughts. Then he began to slow down, to forge a new relation to the sky, to the cosmos; so that his body became a mere stopgap on the way to mystical horizons, to the incomparable promises of fulfilled desire. Now he's terse. I can only imagine how this plays out in the classroom. He's become aloof, a disembodied visionary: The first stage of love.

And when he talks to someone, anyone, he's really talking to her. I know this now. This is how it all started. With his locating her in everyone, in every object, in each moment of time.

The moment of their first brief encounter, for instance. Or *his* encounter with her. She didn't notice him. She was too engrossed in her schedule, attempting to locate the right classroom, there in the corridor. He was meandering from his office to nowhere in particular, walking out the small jitters that accompany him on the first day of class. All the same, he's quite comfortable in his role at this point. People like him. He strolls through the corridor of the stately building with entirely manageable nerves, saying hello to familiar faces. He's enjoying the sensation, a kind of public backstage, limbering up, bobbing his head from side to side, a virile boxer. A performance is only minutes away, in the lecture hall. The crowd sits quietly in anticipation.

Then she appeared to him, standing by the entrance, eyeing her schedule, older than the rest, well-dressed but casual in the way my husband likes. A serious student. And here is where we (in keeping with the self-confessed limitations of his rather lengthy letter) must push beyond casual discourse on the attire of engaging women, of everyday attractions and ordinary beauty. We must raise our consciousness to another level, to a space where words are revealed to be the spurious descriptors that they are. He must have felt, instinctively, with a cosmic prescience, that this woman who was standing before him was pivotal to his fate. This is an instant of momentous proportions, he intuited. He felt it within, in his abdomen to be specific, and in the temporary lack of motor skills. He was immobilized. Others walked around her as though she were a mere object in their way. Only he, in that jubilant moment outside time, discerned her significance. The two of them there. Maurice and the student. The center of the universe. This is where he stepped outside of himself, outside of time, and me.

Two

HE SCANNED THE CLASSROOM. Who are these people? What do they think? Who do they think they are? He formed impressions. But let's imagine his undoing there, quite unusual for a prizefighter of his caliber, as his gaze invariably lands on her, the one who had stopped time only moments before. Fate had transported that illimitable, other world of an instant into his classroom. He breathed with effort and took her in. A committed student, to be sure, a vision, in fact, to melt all pretense, the outline of which blurred other faces and bodies, everything around her. He allowed his gaze to rest on this vision without speaking, lingered there, as his steady, secret consciousness of her became less secret. Such awkwardness that was to eventually bring hazy others back into focus if anything pedagogical was to be salvaged. He stepped back into time. And then he committed errors, mispronounced common names. He tried too hard to maintain his boxer's equipoise. He strutted over to the wall and pressed the button that drops the projection screen. A suave and certainly pragmatic effort, had he been planning to show a video on that first day of class. He barely listened to a student providing introductory background information, his struggle to answer basic questions a series of ruinous abortions. The screen rested quietly, and remained blank, behind him, before the expectant class. Everyone likes a video. He worked hard to remove her from his core awareness.

She stared at him, concentrated but not devouring, as some students are in their need for parental figures when far from home. A stark vulnerability in her countenance nonetheless, but matched by an equally compelling strength. She appeared to be Scandinavian in origin. Or Dutch. Or French. Any of these are excellent choices. She could have passed for a German. Her hair was up, tied back in a taut bun. Pleasant features, to be sure, even in their angularity, and in the severity of her expression there, where time was beginning to sag. An older student amid juveniles.

Her pale complexion: fresh, just not quite inviting. The harshness of Norwegian winters can benumb a personality. A woman inhabiting the floating space between youth and menopause, not unlike me… Incidentally, we don't have children, and at this point, very much in time, it seems unlikely… He was both encouraged and undone by her smile when she found something he said amusing, finally. He was, contrary to the inclemency of the room, in heat. You know what I'm talking about. And the only problem, the only blemish on this remarkable visage, this extraordinary encounter, was that he couldn't read her, how she might have felt as she sat stoically, with her infrequent, nerve-enhancing smile, whether or not she shared his sense of mystery and awe in the light of their beholding one another. He still can't. Hence his departure. A lost man.

It should be apparent that I still sympathize with him, despite the range of transgressions, betrayals. The abrupt disappearance. He's my husband. I love him. This means something to me. I think of what he went through, what he currently endures, wherever he may be, and can't help feeling our shared humanity, our life, in which we've always made a concerted effort to wish only the best for one another, without selfishness and the neurosis of parenting one another. This is what love is at a particularly advanced level. Consciousness. All the great minds and hearts say so. Has he been selfish? Certainly. Has he betrayed me with another? Yes he has, in the discomfited totality that is his mind. And I forgive him. What's left is to understand. I comprehend, empathically, the difficulty of his position, I'm human. It's why I'm willing to accept his devotion to another.

But I don't know her, not yet, not really. This will happen. We should all be concerned when it does.

✄ ✄ ✄

Working with a small ensemble is, in fact, an exceedingly fulfilling affair. A trio, mostly. We don't make much money, so we all teach. Except our cellist, who lives off very little income. We don't understand her. We rarely perform. But we play what we like, generally get along, take a certain masochistic pleasure in our creative differences. We rehearse in a beautiful room at the university. Stone masonry, elegant designs. Downtown energy swarms around our room but doesn't intrude. It's quiet here, attractive. The light is good. Tasteful images adorn the walls, a charming portrait of

Debussy. The piano is in excellent condition. A block from where he, my husband, teaches. In Montréal, the city of joy. Debussy, with his arched eyebrows and oddly angled flat head, looks over us with an air of critical support and encouragement. I fiddle with the insides of the piano, alone in our rehearsal space, nurturing the instrument, waiting for the others to arrive.

When he first encounters her, light is a precious commodity. And even with the sun beaming through windows in the city, it is sometimes impossible to feel warm. The cold is overwhelming and robs the light of its heat. So better to reflect indoors, in a comfortable room. Dream our dreams. Talk to her. Which is what he does at the beginning. With a kind of lightheartedness, an ease of well-being and joy, as the Buddhist says. How reassuring to be so rapt, he thinks. He looks in from a comfortable distance, on his growing infatuation, his spirited, interior dialogue. He sees it, hears it, along with the multitude of aggregates comprising his being at any given moment. Winter is good for this. It nurtures interiority. Summer prompts the body to explode into the open. But we'll get to that. He encounters her again in a corridor, erudition pervading the environment, attractive young students in winter coats and scarves, boots. She's no exception, except that she is. A light unto herself, in his eyes. A beam of luminosity, radiance telling him that his life is about to change, however slowly. With or without dignity.

We complain about the winter here, but really, it ignites euphoria in its perverse way. The city glows with the first snow, interiors quietly retracting, but still speaking to one another in hushed winter phrases. Silent communication is often the superlative method of contact. Or musical evocations, elevated composition in the rehearsal space while the light outside plays upon the snow in an endlessly engaging vision. One's awe fades, of course. Winter can be hard, it takes a toll as months pass. All the more reason to wear one's internal activities on one's sleeve when inspiration strikes. You're a thinker, you have ideas, you're going through something you want others to know, select others. We're all in this together so here it is for all to see. Like me, you need somebody, some thing to expand your centre. It's cold out there. You are not alone.

Three

OUR DAYS TOGETHER in this rupturing milieu are filled with warmth that quickly becomes alienation. We sometimes eat separately. We look up suspiciously upon seeing the other with a plate of something. What is that? one of us asks. The sole diner holds up and tilts the plate, food nearly sliding to the floor. A knowing and distrustful nod follows.

I'm not big on electronic devices. The countless screens that separate us from the real. Maurice was dead set against them, all of them, discounting his own relatively simple-minded laptop. Fearful of how they debilitate social relations, bulldoze attention spans, remove us from the discipline of philosophical thought. Until he met her. Me, I play the piano. Eighty-eight keys, thirty-six in black and fifty-two in white, big, solid wood, wire, the small interior hammers that react to the flesh and blood velocity at which I come into contact with ivory. *Gravicembalo col piano e forte.* An instrument with a singular purpose. I don't require that it go online. It needn't show me videos, connect me to miserable or overly ecstatic peers from kindergarten, or tell me the time in Prague. It's my connection to beauty, the thing that always works.

She rarely spoke in class. Their initial contact beyond that first day was fundamental to the trajectory of his drifting under the window, in his office, music playing in the background, or anywhere the immediacy of his presence wasn't essential. She first reached out to him via email. An opening, a confession. It was hardly indicative of love, or even the mad student crush. She was so sincere in her expression of pleasure in the course, her testimony that she had chosen well, it moved him greatly to think of the isolation in which she was feeling and writing to him. We all secretly fantasize that the object of our desire lives a more or less secluded existence, away from seductive influences; patiently, or perhaps desperately awaiting the gift of our desire. 'And here are some additional thoughts on tonight's discussion that I was too shy to share,' she had suggested in the relative distance of electronic communication. They were insightful, perceptive. She apologized for not being more vocal in class. Such modesty was beautifully touching in light of her age, older than the rest, very close to our own. This was the beginning of what we might call a drilling of the portal into his being. We all know it entered via the cranium, though it felt more like a scooping out of the intestines, he explained in his letter to me. We all know this sensation. The disembowelment, when it takes us unawares and proceeds to enact a slowly unfolding *seppuku*.

He never would have expected it, beyond the mysterious epiphany—love is often a paradox—that stopped him in the corridor and commanded him to wonder who. And when it came, he responded in kind. He got comfortable in the desk chair, wriggled as one does, and wrote with careful glee, measured zeal. 'I'm delighted to hear that you're enjoying the class. And your insights,

I couldn't agree more…' And he was being sincere. Make no mistake. He has never abandoned his sincerity, at least when it comes to her academic performance—I know him well enough to know this, I trust his professionalism and integrity, even now. 'Yes, please do feel free to drop by my office to discuss your future as a scholar', a thoughtful person, the woman who has collapsed the walls of my emotional fortress, enchantress, killer of my logic. These last descriptors ventured no further than his private contemplation.

He responded in the manner of an elder gentleman, an experienced pedagogue, albeit one whose birth date falls within a reasonable number of years relative to her own. He is not stodgy, a dinosaur of an academic. He dresses well. Comfortable street shoes. For even the casual observer it is clear that one need only peel back a layer or two to locate a man whose not so distant youth flourished with street credentials. The street on which you find trendy music clubs and cafés. A nearly obsolete record store. Sushi. At least two sushi restaurants in the neighborhood. There's a park off the street where one can relinquish all responsibilities of the day and vanish into nature when the sun is shining. Or beneath clouds before or after winter has hit hard. This is his turf when not writing or reading philosophy. He's always thinking it, until his citadel of thought took a harder hit than winter gusts afford, temperatures way below freezing. Until this point, he was a bastion of critical theory with too many publications to list. Let's give him some credit for his accomplishments before we snigger at the thought of a philosopher in heat.

All of this I know, of course, from the emails, from his measured responses to her reaching out in the ether, from having scoured his laptop for clues. He left it behind. His email (his password, recently changed, wasn't difficult to figure out, if you know what I mean) tells me things, stories of measured affection and strategy. And the many fragments of scholarship, completed manuscripts that rest elsewhere on the hard drive. He appears to have no need of pornography. But it says nothing of his current location. I remain a potential widow, a grieving woman. I miss him.

Ravel. Chevalier. Merleau-Ponty. Of the big three who wielded his forename in occasionally awkward, often exquisite musical or philosophical productions, only the third is what you would not call purely coincidental. His parents, too, had a vast library, ambition, and career plans for their unborn son that included profound engagement with objects of the mind. Like him, they're gone but not forgotten.

The nature of philosophy – the essential question for him when not staring into a screen, or navigating whatever nowhere geography, whatever hereafter he now calls home—is neither a collection of aphorisms (sound bites from Eastern religion, biblical sayings, Native American wisdom) nor an esoteric self-stroking that occurs in the remote tower of a university. No, he says. It is neither of these. It's a matter of breathing correctly. Breathing thought into the everyday. Critical thought. Forging links between ideas, fresh becomings in the context of a life so complex that our thought, our presence is a mere sheen on this complexity. And yet we are somehow integral to it, we *are* nature, thinking, breathing into the body, he says.

He gives himself over to lengthy considerations of the 'somehow' and the degree to which it might direct any given day. He can't resist the undoing of everything we once took for granted, ideas about self, other people, place and time, and their partial reconstruction into what he and a few of the more daring of his colleagues, at this institution and others, call joy.

He teaches a class on philosophy and literature. Certain members of the literature faculty are resentful. Some of his colleagues in philosophy don't understand. But others generally admire him; he's a beacon of hope for academia. Good people thinking multi-faceted thoughts without the albatross of neurosis and social awkwardness so common to active minds—increasingly rare in this age of technological prowess. Then she—she landed in his philosophy and literature course and now Maurice must bear the reconfiguring of the qualities of goodness and psychological well-being in his life. A weighty matter indeed.

We continued in our way a bit longer. Before things got serious. The everyday life, wife and husband, the two of us more or less alone. We have dinner out. He picks at something on my coat while we're waiting for our table. A subtle gesture that nevertheless speaks to the easy familiarity we share. Apes do it, people do it. We need to pick at one another. This is the closest we've been in a week. He tells me a joke that is infinitely subtle and without malice. It brings levity and warmth to our otherwise fragile condition. What's the soundtrack? I have to override whatever vile Québécois music is issuing from the speakers on the other side of the room. Darius Milhaud: *Sonata No. 1 for Viola and Piano, Op. 240.* A personal favourite. So I turn to face him and seek his lovely smile as further encouragement of our union. We don't have to determine the shape of the next ten years, or how we'll look when we're old together. We don't even need to acknowledge tomorrow, I think. But I need him, now, in this moment, my man, my husband.

His lectures were about to take on the immediacy of singular communication. For the time being, he worked the room in its entirety without losing awareness of her there. Same desk as always. We're such creatures of habit. And really, how convenient this was for him. How nice not to be burdened by classroom topography. He didn't have to think about it. He knew she was there before he took his place at the head of the class, in that spot, hit by that beam of light when the sun chose to radiate through the window during the hour of their meeting. It was invariably in her direction that he rested his attention upon entering and steadying himself at the podium.

He teaches because it's his job, but he enjoys the base line of pedagogy, conversation, the back and forth, to and fro; and the light that sometimes emanates from a student when a realization is made, or from his own triumphant divination in the classroom, his thoughts leading him in a novel direction, an article or monograph idea. The student's insight, always so seemingly offhanded to him and profound that he is reminded of what he adores about his vocation. Other people.

He arrives home early on these evenings, in a wistful state, only slightly agonized. I ask him what's wrong. Nothing, nothing. Fatigue. They made him work tonight. His students were too quiet. 'I had to entertain them. Stones, logs, cows with those empty staring black eyes.' Malice sometimes enters his jokes. I've picked this up from him to some degree and from my peers at the conservatory those years ago, and from my own pedagogy and time with young composers. It's all in the execution. Love them and hate them.

As it turns out, she has a name, a password. At least he knows this much about her. It stood out to him, on his roll, weeks before the semester began. How could it not? But it was only when he called on her that first day and matched it with a face that he became aware of its full significance. In fact, if we're to be completely honest, he knows more about her than this. The Internet is a powerful tool. We'll get to that.

Silke. Contemplate the name. Sit with it for a moment. Then jump to the obvious reference and feel it against the skin. We all know the sensation. It calls out to us. We all need this kind of tactile experience in our lives. Could there possibly be anything to dislike about someone with such a name? Not yet. Her name resists evil. And when applied to her person—her serious, committed studiousness, her forthright innocence even, her hair—we begin to question whether or not there is such a thing as evil. Surely her questionable role as temptress is augmented by his insatiable passion. She is for all intents and purposes benign. Yes. Evil is a figment of humanity's collective imagination. How fortunate that some lone figures occupy the margins of the human community and periodically invite us to weigh the possibility of absolute goodness, beauty and the way that feels to the touch. *Silke.* I weigh the power of such a name; it gets under my skin, too.

We awake in the morning to a colder bedroom than usual. It's still very much winter. Very little has happened beyond the teaching, students, the piano. Sometimes we watch films together, in the evening. Or we listen to music. Naturally, this is my domain, though on occasion he chooses the music. He doesn't play but he has a good ear. I've educated his tastes as he has educated my philosophy. We're good together in this respect. Neither of us has any interest in astrology, though I suspect we would be, at the very minimum, considered helpful partners to one another in light of planetary positions. None of this helps us with the cold, though. The heating system is broken.

What it means is a call, another responsibility to add to the day's responsibilities. 'Please,' I say, 'Will you handle this one?'

Perhaps this is a turning point for me. I know little of names, sacred corridors, at this point in time. All I want is to sleep well. Some warmth in my life. And as much as he too, appreciates a warm bed, the call is superceded by time on the floor, drifting in thought, in the winter light. An entire day goes by and no call is made. Which means another night of added blankets, maybe the flu if we're not careful. This condition would, as any reasonable thinker knows, keep him from seeing her, but he's not thinking like that. He is, rather, grounded in a present that's not quite what religious people mean by presence. And so once again, even the strength of winter pales next to the natural force of a woman whose name connotes that fabric the touch of which stimulates like no other. It is while lying in bed this night, my aggravated sense of feeling alone despite his heavy breathing body and active dream life more or less frozen next to me, myself a shivering body under several inches of barely effective cover, not silk, that I intuit an indiscretion.

Four

WINTER CAN BE HARD, no doubt about it. However, this fact hardly precludes running in the colder months. In addition to teaching music, composing mostly melancholic music on the piano and rehearsing with my ensemble, I'm a committed runner. Nothing stops me. I become a strategist and learn to work with the weather. There are, of course, chic winter running clothes, very expensive. I can afford such items given that collectively my husband and I have disposable income, a low mortgage payment on our lovely condominium and no children. When the weather is entirely too severe I go to a gym with an indoor track. You can imagine the disappointment of all the round-and-round, the lack of scenery, after having grown accustomed to hills and shifting environments over the course of a run on warmer days. But I adapt. I learn to enjoy the static quality, the precision of track running. I know exactly how many miles I've run at my competitive running time. I don't want to run too many miles in this way though, so I tend to run faster when it's cold outside. Short, fast miles on the track. Time starts to mean something there.

Perhaps as a way to balance his time on the floor, he has, surprisingly, begun to join me in the running. He's never been out of shape *per se*. But you can imagine the toll that floor-time might eventually take. He's slowly becoming a runner. Obviously, he has an immense capacity for devotion. We start in the gym with only the barest trace of reserve on his part. He comes to appreciate the way he looks in running attire. We run at a comfortable pace. Side by side, we speak of banal activities, or we discuss the film we watched the previous evening as our legs move in tandem. Sometimes we speed up and then slow down. Such measured sprinting is good for the abdominals, particularly the external oblique muscles. Burning leg muscles. It's called *fartlek* training. It was developed by the Swede Gösta Holmér. I don't know anything else about him, though I do sometimes wonder about Gösta Holmér's taste in music due to his foregrounding of varied pace, much like some music. By the end of most runs, my husband holds a look of deep satisfaction that lasts for minutes, sometimes hours.

Children. Would they have made a difference? Would she have made such an impression had there been a child, a co-created life form that relied on us for sustenance, protection, unconditional compassion? A child requires one's full attention. Of course, classroom time belongs to him, and to her. No one intrudes upon that time, not even a child. That room is sacred space, a *temenos*. Maurice is very fond of the Greeks despite his investment in modern philosophy. There's usually a limit to the freedom children have to be children in adult spaces given the gravity of adult preoccupations. But out of class, surely his paternal instinct would have assumed command, in the domestic realm, at home, in the market, a restaurant when the little one seemed especially well-behaved, or upset about some misdirection. Though these things are hard to gauge, the shifting moods of children, I mean. I have complete faith in my husband's capacity for dutiful fatherhood. He would have been joined in floor-time, the two of them, father and child, rolling and playing, speaking to one another, layers of soft blanket under our baby. 'I've never heard you mock coo,' I might say with some surprise, and proceed to love my husband all the more for the musicality of his engagement with our child, more or less helpless, on the floor beside him.

I suppose it's still possible. Or it was, before he vanished. There was no exotic address mentioned in his letter, no sense of where he might be (on this remote island, in this quiet Scandinavian country), nothing about staying in touch or planning a visit. There was nothing of the sort mentioned in the letter that, at the very least, could have provided me with the assurance that he's okay. Children are not likely at this stage. And it's a pity. Because I'm reaching the age that communicates to a woman – 'the thing you are built to do, that has nothing to do with music and running and attending pleasurable social events in such a fine, active city, is about to expire as a possibility. It's not my intention to stack on the pressure; culture, parents, take care of that,' my age says, in its generally polite manner. 'I'm just suggesting, in keeping with the normative constraints of a life span, that if you're going to do this, it should happen soon. Otherwise there might be consequences. I don't need to go into these with you. You're smart, a terminal MFA in music from a prestigious conservatory,' my age observes. 'You understand these things.' Otherwise, the totality of years offers a steady stream of congratulations on the running, the excellent diet, the never having smoked a cigarette and very little drinking. Though abuse of the latter is not entirely out of the question at this point.

⚘ ⚘ ⚘

Many speak of running as a mechanism used to cultivate endurance beyond the pavement, the rocky and root-laden trail. I agree with this. I've endured countless moments alone at the piano, pencil in hand, attempting to place notes on and in between the lines, feeling the urge to stop, put it down, look at a magazine, eschew guilt. Instead I keep moving, my running experience asserts itself, and I shift to a pen. This way the marks are permanent, intensifying the composition in the face of fatigue. Or while evaluating student work, which can be overwhelmingly poor and formulaic, I keep grading, listening. The running has educated my ability to go long and to push through adversity.

⚘ ⚘ ⚘

There was the slightest break in the weather today. Still far from that day when the sun manifests warmth and the temperature climbs by as much as ten or fifteen degrees, inviting people to leave their homes and to wear the warmer temperature on their faces, to make children frolic. We're not there yet. But the extreme cold has lifted just enough to inspire an outdoor run. He borrows some of my winter gear. He looks good in it. A slick, moving philosopher, he seems to take pleasure in his appearance. Sure, why not. Enjoy yourself. Let's enjoy this run, our bodies, together, husband and wife.

An experienced runner may not really settle into a run until the third or fourth mile. This is when it hits me today, that moment of elation. I can go forever, I understand the weightier principles of Buddhism in this hallowed moment. I am one with my surroundings, all people. Even the obese, the mass consumers of inconceivably terrible music, every self-important representative of excess and mediocrity. We are of one cloth in our collective suffering and possible redemption. I nod to him, as though he too is floating over the pavement in silent dreams and equanimous relations. On the contrary, Maurice is suffering. And this is fine, very fine. It's all part of the process of settling in, getting to know yourself through physical exertion, a kind of de-personalization. The hill in front of us actually takes us alongside the mountain at the center of the city, part of its incline affording lovely views. It'll be difficult for him. It's difficult to lose one's personality with such vertical abruptness. I reach over and feel the back of his neck. He smiles with effort, begins to lean into the hill. I've taught him proper running technique. Landing on your toes burns the calves at first, a sore day ahead of him tomorrow, to be sure. He leans in further, head down. I'm proud of him, how delightful that we can share this. Tonight, a nice dinner, no infant noises to disturb us, something uncomplicated to watch on television.

He keeps pushing himself. I'm proud of him. I witness the process that I myself undergo when racing, the ongoing push toward the finish line, your body, your age crying 'please stop, you want to, it's easy, just stop, you'll feel better.' But you know this last suggestion is a lie, so you utilize your last drop of energy, fuelled earlier by snack dates and a moderate lunch, detoxifying tea. You cross the line exhausted, but triumphant. Your time was excellent…

He keeps pushing, leaning in. He doesn't need my touch now. In fact, what I come to realize is that he doesn't need me at all. It strikes me instantaneously, with blunt force, his psychological ploy of forging a completed path up the hill. If he makes it to the top of this excruciating, life-defying gradient, she will one day be his. Silke. His inspiration, his prodigal muse. He wears her name branded under the *swoosh* of his fleece top, in the heart region, on the entirety of his person, really. He's running for her, trying to impress her with his body. If he makes it to the top, the cosmos will soon reward him with the object of his adoration, he thinks. I bet he plays such games in numerous life arenas. In retrospect, I know this is what he was thinking. He's a forceful thinker, he can think under the most arduous of circumstances. The cloth from which we are cut isn't the same at all. Mine, a soft but durable fabric, practical, always up-to-date. His, of a lustrous fiber that tempts the skin into believing in its longevity, supple and compelling to the touch.

He makes it to the top, to where our course evens out. He is dreaming of her. He is panting and being deeply internal and wishing I was someone else.

At home, we put on a pot of tea and stretch next to one another in the living room, our limbs touching as we reach further into the burn.

Five

THURSDAY AFTERNOON, I closed the door to my office and wept. Crying is good, healthy. Like running, it releases endorphins and lowers stress levels. It's detoxifying. Tears born of sorrow carry more toxins than those born of irritants, onions, or pepper spray. We should cry more. We laugh too much, and with malice. Crying removes unwanted particles from our bodies. All the same, I wept behind closed doors so as to avoid a stir in the corridor. There's been enough of that around university corridors. I was losing him. The man with whom I exchanged vows, vows we wrote together. I couldn't understand his absence of late. *To love and to honor. To celebrate, respect.* He was becoming a distant star, the coils that tethered us were unfurling. *To uphold in consciousness. To communicate clearly, affectionately. To co-create.* The uncertainty and lack of communication between us was starting to hurt. This would be the first of several such episodes in my office, at home, on an otherwise deserted street, in the well-sanitized bathroom of a bustling café.

Maurice found weights in a dumpster near our condominium. He began using them religiously. A further detoxification of unwanted fat. How eccentric of him! Ordinarily, he would just buy something he wanted. We're not particularly ashamed of our money and I'm sure he would agree that we have the right perspective on it all. What is money? Cosmic currency, it's always available. And when it's not, we are not excessively attached to material objects, exotic travel, over-priced restaurants. But he's digging through trash. He seems emboldened by spontaneity of late, and less energized by philosophical speculation. Theory is secondary now. He's a 'now moment' kind of man these days. I tell him so over dinner (the heat is back on, he called, eventually) and we progress to an after-dinner *amaretto* on the sofa and a mutual elucidation on the meaning of time and presence.

I tell him how much he's hurting me by his absence. 'I'm right here,' he says. He reaches to touch my arm. He tells me a joke that infects me with benign laughter. Then I regain my composure. 'It's not enough,' I say. He leans back. For a long time we both stare at the walls. We stare out the window, into the absence of light. The soft-crackling stillness of snow in the dark. Eventually he looks at me and pats his heart. I still don't know what this means, though I take it as a sign of endearment.

He said, at the end of another day, a particularly easy day, 'it's wonderful to see you now.' I remember sensing the warmth emerge from my chest and spill out into other parts of my body when he said this. An overall sensation of being met, warm feeling cognition. Something as simple as that, provoking me in such a way, does not make me weak or gullible. No, I love my husband. He makes me feel. People have this effect on one another. Especially when occupying the calm center of a natural disaster.

I was wrong. He's working on a new philosophy project. The body. Sexuality. Performing the sexual body. I know a great deal about the musical body, the physiology of listening, ergonomics. His topic is outside my field. And really, it's outside his as well. But that's a philosopher for you, always thinking, always breathing life into new ideas. He speaks of it one day, on one of the rare afternoons that we're home together without his drifting into the spaciousness of no thought, Mahayana emptiness, or pointed thoughts of her. The body as constructed by social formulas—nothing new there—but his intention to excavate the meaning of an object as vital as one's body in the face of that object's decentralization... What is a body once it becomes unanchored in a panorama of estrangement, or to be even more dramatic, pummeling desire? This is the central question. 'Philosophy, being the primary instrument in the removal of a core, or rather the exposure of that core's absence, thus propagating the sexual self and its body as an extension of that self, or vice versa.' I read this on his laptop. What is sex in the end? Another big question for him. He still has a great deal to work out. Ultimately, he says, it comes down to the phenomenology of love. Strong words for the nearly departed.

I imagine him in the classroom, discoursing on the sublimation of authors in love: he would have asked his students, his discourse directed at one student in particular, 'Is it fair to persecute the author who frames with such precision a portrait of desire? What if there are insurmountable obstacles? What if the object of his affection lies on the opposing side of a chasm that is far too distant to reach, as it does for our protagonist? Her impending marriage to another, her propriety. The poor German boy in the blue coat, the always defeated. Perhaps literature is all he's got. Maybe words are his only refuge,' my husband would have concluded, a little dejected, his head down, staring at the floor. In fact, Silke conveyed the content and the nuances of his pedagogy with a measured tonality when she spoke to me, after the fact, in my university office. After he vanished for good, body and spirit. We'll get to this. She was wary of me, there was no question, but remained forthright in her testimony under the eventual spotlight of his, and our, predicament—the enigma of his disappearance, his giving up, in the end. Not unlike a protagonist for whom death looms large.

She wrote to him, again, out of nowhere, with the sole purpose of making a recommendation. Something from her own catalogue of interests, a book, something he knew instantly that he would devour as though it were her body, her self, hair down, nearly touching her slim shoulders, being offered.

And here, for the first time, he questioned what it meant—her reaching out beyond the classroom dynamic of student and teacher, through electronic mail, succinct words on the screen. What is she saying? Is there something beneath the surface? Is there anything to read *into* here? Or does she simply mean what she says? Here is this phenomenon, perhaps you would enjoy it—literalism is such a rarity these days outside of religious and rightwing political discourse. He wanted to believe that she was scheming, that she lacked no substance, no understanding of subtlety, of the many fine gradations of meaning. And why not? Look at him. Well-aged, his having aged like a gentleman, a poet, a Viking poet, winning the war over the deterioration of cells, his mind still a blade slicing through ideas. I've already described his attire. Did I mention his walk? There was a point, many years ago, when he entertained the prospect of becoming a model. This went nowhere, though the walk he practiced from room to room in his apartment at the time stuck. He walks like a model, a male feline. He exaggerates the walk for me, in the privacy of our home, on occasion, the embellishment having toned down somewhat, in light of Flesh changing density, the mostly imperceptible manifestations of unwanted fat over months, years. But now he runs.

What does it mean, her extending herself over the border, the no-nonsense arrangement of I write and you grade? It means something, he told himself.

Her next message, several days later, was a short, succinct reply. She didn't address any of the comments he had made on the book she had recommended him. She had no comeback; she failed to acknowledge the cleverness of his humanity. He is, let us be honest, nearly always at the head of the classroom, casting his words into a discursive pool of insight, humor, inviting his listeners, friends, or colleagues, to take a dip, most of whom are happy to dive in completely nude. They enjoy his manner, his conversational aplomb, as do I, splashing around in his word pool. But she was not interested in swimming. She had nothing clever to say; she made no effort. There was no sense of her taking pleasure in the sensuality of words. Her message was indicative of a younger generation's abbreviated correspondence. But the thought of her in swimwear, wet and dripping, was entirely too much for him.

I'm currently exploring digital technology. The cat sits loyally beside me. Have I mentioned the cat? That's one male out of two left in this household. I'm afraid to let him out now, which has meant educating a sensitive creature, also young at heart but approaching middle age, in the ways of indoor toiletry. My paranoia may be his and our undoing. But I can't lose anyone else in my life at the moment. I can't make it through that. He sits at my foot, by my slipper, the heel of which dangles above the hardwood floor. He's too old to bother tapping at it. From the computer speaker a Swiss woman tells us about Dvořák. I'm scrolling through Internet radio stations. Fascinating. The cat seems to appreciate the Swiss German voice but remains unconvinced by Dvořák and his music. Felines, I discovered on the Internet, are sometimes eaten and killed for fur in Switzerland, so it's ironic that he would prefer a potential murderer over Dvořák. For my part, I too appreciate the woman speaking on another continent, and that this marvel can happen instantaneously via computer technology. It's all so extraordinary, the mysterious umbilical cord connecting us to music, pictures, people in front of their computers, searching through time.

I joke about the cat's anthropomorphic qualities, its manhood, the ironies of its life or its distaste for Czech composers, but I want to be clear about something. I need him. He's more to me than a narrative device, a source of levity amidst what must by now be perceived as an imperiled chronicle of loss. He looks at me tenderly when he's hungry and when he craves attention. We settle into restfulness together at night, when he moves away from my feet and closer to my head on the sofa, or in the bed that is now larger than it needs to be. Plenty of room for the two of us there now, but still he's never lost the desire to tuck into the fold of my neck, even after all these years. He's someone who knows me.

Six

WE WALK ARM IN ARM along the waterfront, on *Rue de la Commune Est*. What a strange thing to do here! Few come to the Old Port except tourists. But today is still winter and the cold bites into your face. Tourists don't like the cold. They prefer summer and flip-flops. It was my idea to share a walk and his idea to tour the edge of the city. We're alone here. The city center, home to our university, the many people, muted, industrial sounds, a nice compliment to the static body of water. Everything is grey-blue, an aqua-quiet that pushes us even further into ourselves, into the delicate silence of the day. We make small talk nonetheless. He tells me how much he can appreciate choral music when the mood is right. An obvious affinity. And yet I now recall this discussion with great clarity, the earnestness with which he spoke, the seeking, the meandering of his associative thoughts attempting to communicate musical feeling, the sensation that such music incarnates. I, in turn, explain his appreciation. What it is about the human voice that draws us out, or in, that special union of voices that makes us weep, or feel closer to whatever we conceive as sanctity in our midst. That even a single voice can do this to us.

All this talk of the human machine reminds me of a decisive moment in their correspondence. There was another casual message, an additional recommendation on her part. A few microscopic shreds of information as to who she is, what she's about, what moves her, if anything. It's difficult to tell with a woman like this, while I, as you should know by now, am anything but vague on the subject of what moves me. He was quietly exuberant, I imagine. Until he got to the end of the message. She told him where she lives, invited him for coffee sometime. Whereupon he became less quiet in the estuary of his thoughts, where the present moment and future exaltations mixed to concoct an elixir. She suggested he drop by, anytime, really. Enter her home. The lab of her alchemy. Fireworks exploded and his body tightened. The pleasure waves began their addictive proliferation through the body. But the climax was yet to come. Keep calm. Savor the moment. Read on. 'My boyfriend and I,' she wrote, 'we love a good coffee.' This must have fallen, or erupted off the screen. 'We'd love to see you.' *We*. A dark, intrusive monolith of a pronoun disfiguring the landscape of an exhilarating proposal.

A loss. Chest pain. His guts emptied out onto the floor, or imploded within the collapsing sack of his lower torso. She's not who he thought she was. The loss of dreams, his identity in her, the self he had fortified around her, at one with her, is now ravaged. It's over.

Best not to laugh. Best to unlock the gates to benevolence. Withhold judgment. He had imagined her alone in life. We all imagine such things. A serious, quiescent figure, alone in a room, quietly negotiating the fact that we ultimately live and die alone. With his mind's eye he saw her in her home, with something poignant to listen to on the stereo, or watching thoughtful films alone in the night. The things singular people do to give life substance. Creating art when not busy reading, which he imagined her doing curled up on a sofa, her legs mostly covered by a blanket, a bare shoulder where her shirt collar is falling indifferently down an arm. Her hair is down rather than up, as it often is in class. She's a tea drinker, a glass of wine in the evening. He can taste the wine before it touches her lips; then it's the lips he tastes.

But none of this held together. It was a fabrication that he would now have to banish from his dreams. His drifting beneath the window becomes a different enterprise now. She is not alone in the world, she doesn't need him. All these things she does in concert with another, as it turns out. A younger man, younger than me, he must have thought. Maurice began the process of elevating and then tearing down the boyfriend. He works out. He has excellent hair. How could he not? Probably not too bright, though. Midlife for this inadequate boy is thousands of motorcycle miles away. He probably drives a motorcycle... Of course, of course he does, this strapping young insurgent, this young Marlon Brando. A massive loss, a torment to think of her being touched, contacted in the intimate way of couples, by a young Brando.

Then everything was different. Relations to objects. Which is what she would become to him, a separate thing, in the sad recognition of another. He would covet her differently now, the professor; desperately, in the classroom, in the refuge of his home, on lonely walks. His dreams would be populated with monsters. He would see her everywhere and nowhere. All places are changed once one is forced to carry the weight of a word on one's back.

Before we were married, he preferred the term partner to boyfriend or girlfriend. The latter seemed too juvenile, too teen-oriented. Or like the fifty-year-old woman who chain-smokes, wears sweatpants year-round, drinks excessively, a smoker's voice, and refers to her better half, a real winner of a man, a greaser, as her boyfriend. Partner is much more dignified, he would say. And then we were betrothed. We underwent a ceremony attended by philosophers and musicians, family, others from the miscellaneous category. It was very simple and quick. No fanfare, no speeches. No cake. But the vows, written weeks prior on a late Spring evening when the cat was still a kitten and people had already begun dining on terraces, were eloquent and meaningful. Now it's unclear what we should call each other. I use husband for the sake of convenience. Ex? Former spouse? My vanquished half.

But he wrote back immediately. What he said and what I suspect he wanted to say.

'Oh yes, how interesting, what a small world, we live so close by...' *We.* 'Our neighborhoods bleed into one another. We, my wife and I. My wife. I have one. A musician, a composer. A teacher at the university, like me. She's lovely, I bet you'd like her. Beautiful music fills our home, a pianist. I'd be happy to stop by, you're so close. But you can leave the boyfriend out of it, just so we're clear. He can't possibly deserve you. He's a looser, a jerk, a solar system away from your league. Think about what you're doing.'

Her response—it's a quick back and forth, a sunless seesaw—was ambiguous. She seemed surprised. 'I see,' she said. And then: 'Maybe I can take a music class with your wife, with your recommendation.' Full stop. This, this strange statement and then nothing. No sign out. The last sentence just ended, blunt force. That's how it is with the younger generations. The days of inspired correspondences that occupy shelves in university libraries are long gone.

Consider then, his ultimate realization, this moment at the core of his pathos, the moment having slowly evolved out of classroom time and detonated in simple, confessional words on a screen, that the only way to communicate his developing feelings for her given the many obstacles, the boyfriend, the wife, professional ethics, would require enormous skill and foresight. The only acceptable manner in which to voice his feelings would be to speak to her in class, through texts, through teaching and in the immediate presence of other students. I need you, he would say through the conterminous voices of literature and philosophy. You've entered that part of me that yearns to open, a rose petal in nascence. A flower that now slams shut in the darkness of your absence when I don't hear from you, when I think of the inane motorcyclist in your life. As certain flowers wilt in the night. This is how far it's come. I think of you here from my privileged position at the lectern, and I think of indescribably beautiful music, a chorus of voices. Or the moment of grasping a link between grandiose ideas, radical notions. *Et voilà...* My Maurice could have give his life for hers. Believe it. This sudsy notion wasn't beyond him. Silke, he would trumpet, your smallest word, your single voice, hear this, has awakened me. Here in our private *marivaudage,* our own secret dismantling of time, he would say to her in the classroom through the vaulted intimations of others.

Imagined talk in the space of lectures, sacred, but no less real as vented through the channels of other speakers—philosophers, literary or mythical characters, feeling and pronouncing for all of us. Maurice and the object of his affection, surrounded by others who were, it must be said, equally deserving of his attention. And yet he knew that hers would be the desk and the body and the inquiring mind that received the tender might of all he said and of his every move in the classroom. Through the intricate web of texts, each allusion and proclamation for her alone. On desire, craving, becoming, becoming-imperceptible, shorn of time... The foci of literature and philosophy. The guiding principle of which, animating his every pointed instruction, its girth, height and center, would be love, or the death thereof.

I hold him in my arms. He seems despondent. The night has worn on and we're all a little ragged. Together on the sofa, the cat beside us, my men, tucked in for the night. His grip on my body is non-committal, but I continue holding. I need him. The wind howls outside. I pull the blanket up around our legs, all eight of them. A film has begun, this should take him out of his corrosive thoughts, give him something else to think about.

I can't imagine what's bothering him this moment.
It's still winter. The film looks bleak, Scandinavian.
He will have to hold onto me too if he wants this
configuration on the sofa to last.

Seven

SILKE.

What's the soundtrack? A difficult proposition, to be sure. What music accompanies her at any given moment, defines her, in the way that film music accompanies and helps sculpt the visual, her movement through life? As much as he would like to believe that her listening revolves around graceful, thoughtful music, I doubt that this is the case. People who tap inane, abbreviated phrases into electronic devices by way of communication, as their sole means of communication, don't listen to thoughtful music. They don't really listen at all. But that's another discussion, a journal article, a scholarly monograph. I'm being cynical, I know, which weakens my position.

Maurice Ravel, *Boléro*. How could it be anything else? A triumphant march through life. Another cliché, it's true. Not even a particularly great piece, really. But bear in mind that I'm still being more than generous here.

Silke.

Even at this early stage, he seeks to put her into perspective. He tries to contextualize the phenomenon of Silke as one woman among many. He endeavors to locate her on a vast continuum of women, an infinitesimal number of whom, in the grand scheme, he's known. Or others he will never know except through contact with the screen. Their celluloid or digital surfaces, characters they play in film. He rarely watches television now. This strategy seems to work temporarily. Until it doesn't, when an embodied Silke enters the classroom. Or on those erratic, numinous occasions when he sees her in a different space, where she is so much more than an actress or a memory, where that stretch of road, that café, becomes sacred, where common gestures and neuroses are pleasantly magnified. When time slows to a vermicular crawl and he thinks about her too long and too hard.

Or when, after a late night of perusing nothing special on the Internet (he is trying to become more like her) he invites me over to the machine the following morning to watch something. 'Incredible,' he says. 'I don't mean to ruin your day, but watch this.' How can it possibly be good news?   You know how it is when people make such requests. One of our favorite actresses, as it happens, French by way of Switzerland, on screen here, but not acting in the conventional sense. She's singing on a television show, French music. She's still beautiful, you'll get no argument from me there. She walks steadily toward the camera from the back of the stage. She carries herself like the model she plays in the film. Her voice is fine, just fine. But the music! Let's not mince words. The French, whom we both love, along with those who claim a French heritage in our own province here, get many things right. Fashion, literature, philosophy, food. The list is long and perverse. But where they go astray, and please keep in mind that this is being exceedingly generous, is in their popular music. Everyone but the French can hear it. Why don't they? Why does an actress of this caliber not know this? Why does she contribute to the problem? Why is she part of the problem? I don't know. Another academic undertaking, a theoretical and perhaps, an empirical study...

We look at each other in disbelief and bow our heads. A moment of dejected camaraderie shared between us.

His intention was to see his student and all the finely woven fabric of his desire on this scale whereby she pales in comparison to all the lovely women of the world. Actresses, writers, philosophers, musicians, models who see the world at its grandest, its most hedonistic. Aviators. Or even savvy politicians. All on video. All of whom reduce her, even if temporarily, to a position of provinciality, a pleasing but uncultured wood-nymph whose contribution to the world would never amount to more than a few academic essays by an inconsequential being in the universe of people living and dying on the backs of motorcycles.

But Maurice knows that even heroes are susceptible to the vicissitudes of life and death. They become jealousy and hangnails. They commit the ultimate sin of boredom, as the poet says. They sing. And he knows as much as anyone else that attempting to abstract what cannot ultimately be abstracted—a valuable woman, a student, an intelligent, remarkable being—is a fallacy. He thus fails to escape her allure, her immanence. A singular but commanding expression of the world closes in on him again. He stops watching French films for the time being. He drifts into weightless contemplation of the one, very much alive, for whom we would give up everything.

⚓ ⚓ ⚓

I don't listen solely to classical music. I'm not like that. We all know these people. And we know that they rarely if ever cross the border into modernity. No. For them it's the giants or nothing. I won't rehearse the names, you know who I'm talking about. One of the pleasures of working with the ensemble is that we play what we want. We don't have to cater to sponsorship or patronage. If we want to play Schoenberg then that is precisely what we do. But ultimately, I understand these people who eschew the non-classical world, who in their mild manners detest the non-classical, the non-traditional. When you've cultivated a sensibility to that degree, to the degree of the *Requiem*, for example, sincere appreciation of that other music, pop, can only feel degenerate.

But I still appreciate a good hook, a handsome guitarist. Forget an overcrowded music festival, but yes, I'm happy to join you in an intimate club setting. Dancing is a delicate negotiation. The classically-trained rarely know what to do with their bodies on the margins of the instrument.

But I have an excellent Pht body, well-tuned and taught like the strings of my piano. Hopefully you can say the same. That's what running does for us. I can play the piano and run for hours at a time. I teach as well. Some afternoons you find me in one of the numerous cafés near the music department. Composition, piano, music theory: these are the subjects our discussions. Or we share the more or less personal details of our lives. I like people. I congregate with students and colleagues, for better and for worse. My public persona isn't especially different from the woman who dangles a slipper, generally loves and appreciates the cat, or hovers over domestic space. Given the larger surroundings of our city of parks and francophone preoccupations, it's easy to step away from myself. I frequently become immersed in the urgency of the city. The countless men and women around me, my inconsequential self among their immeasurable numbers. It would be a pleasure to look and to play like the incomparable Hélène Grimaud, to live in the spotlight, receive flowers and adulation, to be a commanding omnipresence on the Internet, but this is not the case, and that's fine, just fine. Incidentally, my name is Lucille. And I know exactly who I am.

Eight

AS IT HAPPENS, her initial essay was solid. 'First rate. Top fucking shelf,' in his words. I don't curse often. I hope you don't either. My *grand-mère* used to say cursing is for stupid people. But my husband isn't stupid. Nor apparently is his student. There were a few minor flaws in the essay, nothing that experience won't dissolve. This obviously amped up the terms of engagement. He could have forgotten her had she been a mediocre mind. He accepts, but has little patience for unskilled thought, converts to sound-bite theology, politics, lazy thinkers. He could have enjoyed her beauty while maintaining the emotional distance between student and teacher that, in fact, often makes the teacher all the more appealing. This is what he should have done. What people commonly do in this kind of situation.

✄ ✄ ✄

He took note of the first time she raised her hand in class. He examined this movement, the shape of her uplifted arm, in the brief instant before responding, the slender but firm extension of her hand in the air. A pale lengthening into the cosmos, the shape of her fingers, floating there above the heads of nameless others, he penciled hastily on a slip of paper at the lectern so as not to forget. I found it later, the slip of paper. Elegant muscle and the tapering in at the wrist, where her fingers began their reach. The fingers that touch. In class, he paused. He said her name. 'Silke?' He heard himself say this aloud. He recorded her comments on the inevitability of power dynamics between two people living in intimacy, a sudden revelation, an unexpected eruption of her personal experience, there in the classroom. He knew it and she knew it. Others may have noticed, thought about their own relations in that moment. It didn't matter. Silke operating in the world of men, in close proximity to very fortunate men indeed— this is what mattered.

Silke.

It sounded, when he repeated the name in the

quiet of our home later that evening, alone in his office, like an evocation. Maurice, the great magus, a High Priest of some secret society, an esoteric coven, conjuring up ghosts, objects of desire. In class, in the world bereft of magic and heavy with the weight of sturdy, uncompromising relations, *Silke* heard her name and felt the implication of its living in his mouth nonetheless and of her own power relations that had nothing to do with him, not yet.

Silke who protects herself, a fierce guard to the entrance of her life, except when she doesn't. When she lets slip small insights, crumbs of plenty.

There was a coherence in the rolling fantasy that stemmed from her name, an ordering of her person and her power into confident narratives.

⚔ ⚔ ⚔

He searches for her on the computer at night. But the Internet can't satisfy his need for concrete joy in a world beyond his philosophy. I also spend time at the computer, looking for Silke. But we'll get to that. Scattered information was all that he could find. That he was stalking her only broke through the buffers of his self-awareness after the fact, when it was time to leave, write a monumentally detailed letter, his confession. No forwarding address, no information available online as to his whereabouts. Once it came time to vaporize like—how might a proponent of literature and philosophy put it?—like a mist burned off by the first light of eternal daybreak.

That day she raised her hand and he said her name for the first time was quite possibly the same day I waited for him outside his office on a surprise visit after my rehearsal went late. We'd go home together, I thought. We'd sit across from each other on the metro without speaking. He'd make a face at me. I'd wink back.

But immediately following class, Silke exited with her customary speed, leaving him to a weekend of fantasy and computer consultations. Into the public domain. She was gone. I waited for him there with a wrapped package in my hands, gourmet chocolates from a local chocolatier. But I could tell he was clearly put off, unnerved by my presence there, minutes after their class had ended. It had never been a problem before, my meeting him at his office. Now it was a problem.

She may still have been in the general vicinity. It didn't matter because her aura still resonated there. In retrospect, I know this. Her aura haunting the front of his office, in the corridor, on campus, on the metro. Our home. The cosmos. Everywhere is sacred now. Which makes me, if you'll allow for some small modicum of melodrama, a heretic.

Sometimes he divided the students into groups. He observed her among the others, her interlocution, listened for the singular, velvety tone of her voice among other, chirpy student voices. Periodically, he made out a word or a phrase that, naturally, made him lean into the students, as one might lean into a steep hill while running. What did she just say? If only he was closer. And all of it, her comportment, the chit-chat once the students fleshed out their topic, her being there, it all belonged to her group. This incomparable pleasure that the others hardly recognized as such and thus did not deserve.

Jealousy. It's the wrong word. Envy is more appropriate. He would contemplate the difference between these terms, staring out the window, looking over the desks, the bodies. If given the opportunity, he would likely have exchanged the privilege of teaching for the opportunity to share that group with her. To be her equal, every week, a student, twice a week. Obviously, it was her quiet laughter from within this small, enclosed circle of others that pained him the most.

She never asked, who are you? What do you value? No. Only increasingly brief electronic messages, rarely a moment together before or after class. So he endeavored on occasion to supplement the big ideas in the classroom with details of his personal life for her benefit. She didn't ask, but he was going to tell her anyway. And before the entire class. Maybe he went too far. The time he spent in Scandinavia, the drinking he did there, nudity in the sauna. He shared episodes from his childhood, the near-miss with modeling. He mentioned his ex-partners and the roster of break-ups. The story of his young nephew dancing around one evening in his *grand-mère's* underwear. Such anecdotes that may have been uncalled for, that make a lover laugh. But she was not his lover. Nor were the other twenty-nine students whose questioning looks he noticed and then ignored.

In the morning, we nudge each other periodically without saying very much, after I return from a run, alone. We don't do this together anymore. Though the morning is nice. I nudge him harder than he expected and this brings a mirthful reaction on his part. He stops what he's doing and asks my thoughts about brunch. He never does this, he barely thinks about food. I enjoy cooking, mixing ingredients. One would think that he has an affinity for following recipes, logic, but no. His philosophical interests lie elsewhere. His suggestion of brunch is a positive, a productive thing, I say. He even gets into the shower with me to facilitate the process. What's the soundtrack? George Frideric Handel, *Water Music*. Our bodies squish together in a remote but familiar way, our hair in our faces, mixed shampoos. I take hold of his member and he massages shampoo into my scalp. He asks me to turn around so he can get the back and his semi-erect member squishes against my bottom. It feels nice. Nothing else happens in the shower. Afterwards, we dry our own bodies, move to the bedroom, and dress for brunch.

Nine

FEBRUARY WAS A BLISTERING TOUR through the hardest month of winter. Valentine's Day—what's that? A simulacrum, to put it in theoretical terms. It never happened. It was merely televised.

Winter inches toward spring. There's very little difference between January and early March here. The teeth of freezing cold that bit into your flesh and hit bone have been retracted somewhat, but the brown slush of snow and ice is still everywhere, you can still fall. You still have your winter legs, the unique sense of balance we cultivate here between October and April. It once snowed in June. And then the freeze really lifts, and the buoyancy of the city snaps into action with people strolling, festivals of all varieties, warm air. But not yet. We'll get there.

Montréal. Where weather fosters interiority. Last week I saw a man reading Dostoyevsky on the bus, on my way to rehearsal. On the way home, I saw another, a woman, reading Dostoyevsky on the metro. This is Montréal. One travels with great Russian writers, continental thinkers. Nothing wrong with getting down into the thick of things. The only obstacle is your stop at the next block, the next station. And even then you can continue reading if you're the type of person to read and walk. But you're probably not. Be careful walking regardless. And take comfort in the fact that the temperature is slowly rising.

In a reversal of order of all things seasonal, he was soon lecturing on death in class, he told me. Imagine him, a pacing feline, a word-warrior with a target:

'Death is inherent to any literary undertaking… why? Think. Harness your powers of concentration. Silke?' (He rarely called on students willy-nilly, he preferred volunteers but I imagine him feeling feisty on this day, full of verve, the topic meant something to him).

'Because, you say, and as the text suggests, all plots move deathward,' (she would have said these words with her own confidence, her own spurt of gusto).

'*Oui, absolument!*' (He rarely spoke French in the Anglophone class but as the language of verve *par excellence*, it obliged him). 'The plot, the life situation, yes, it moves toward death with an able-bodied swiftness in the grand and even in the little schemes of time. What is time? Death.

'But consider the metaphor,' he continued. 'Transformation, in time, of time and self. And the differences between characters, their choices, their predicaments. Everyone dies. This we know. The human skull on the desk of a seventeenth century scholar. But those who die a figurative death, those who die daily, as the Bible admonishes us, tend to die more gracefully. Have you noticed this? Do you know what I'm talking about? A kind of shedding, a skinning of the self that prepares one for the final acknowledgement of our ephemerality. Reptiles. The narrative arc, deathward. Even as the pallid noise of everyday culture seeks to drown us in arrested development. Stasis is the real tragedy here. Listen to this, its musicality. Stasis is the only tragedy. It behooves one to engage in motion. To follow all the microscopic becomings of the heart.'

Unbeknownst to him, she had been elated by his calling on her, and by her immediate, improvised response, which was the correct response. All plots move deathward. The seriousness in her expression, her tone of voice, she must have been very beautiful in this moment. The solemnity of her features operating in tandem with the glow I now recall illuminating my office, when she sat before me to inquire about him, to express care. Her private celebration, in the classroom, and later, in her own home that evening, of knowing she had said something that pleased him. I wish, for his sake, that he had been privy to her elation then and there.

Now on the subject of shampoo and showering, let me say that it doesn't escape my attention, the way he has of alternating shampoos. One is cheap, for dandruff, a generic brand even, while the other is more expensive, with exotic properties, fashionable shampoo. Something I gave him. He never buys things like this for himself, but he uses it regularly, I know. Twice a week to be specific: the two days of the week he gets to see her. I shower after him. The bottle I gave him is always covered in drying bubbles, shampoo fizz, on these days. I notice things like this and I see the meaning in potential symbols and a sacred routine in the shower. He consecrates himself on those mornings. He's already with her by the time he's lathering up and smelling like a new man. It's his way of being with her, making her part of his day outside the fact of their sharing a room together for an hour and fifteen minutes twice a week. And he wishes to look his best. We all do what we can. I know. I know a lot about men and women at this point.

His trial in the wake of meeting Silke was to levitate, every second of every day, on a *"cloud of unknowing,"* above the fray of quotidian concerns. The title of an important book that he once shared with me. You should read it. But as it turned out, I was not alone in my discovery of *petite* domestic disturbances. Some more information on him of which Silke remains happily unaware: occasionally he develops an unseemly wart on his right hand. Nothing that alters his appearance to the point of grotesquery, but prominent enough to intrude upon his self-stylization in light of her. He applies a cream when this happens, and then forgets about the cream once the imperfection returns to the cellular murk from which it first emerged. Classic memory repression. But they always return: the wart, his memory, and the cream to give him yet another opportunity to pick at himself during the drifting, the researching, the floating, while the wart grows into a dark, vibrant, purple knoll on his hand. At the time of its last manifestation, while searching for the cream again he found a zip bag of sexual paraphernalia. My zip bag. No big deal. He knew it was there. It all pertained to him, to us, something to celebrate, at least when our marriage included reciprocal sexual behavior. Sometime ago that was.

He looked there anyway, for the cream. One never knows where these things might end up. The condoms he found were old, a product of the early years of marriage. Our initial, mutual reluctance to have children. The mood-altering pill, the pain in the uterus IUD… I would rather not. I would rather not use condoms either, but there are steps one must take to avoid children if one so wishes. You know what I'm talking about. But as it turned out, not all of the condoms were as old as that, or so it appeared to him, as old as the era of sex between us. There were two—they often come in threes—that looked newer than the rest. Let's check the expiration date. The current year.

He asks me about it, in that delicate way of his. Words accompanied by a sincere smile, a moment of levity, a joke. A man is searching through the bathroom cabinets and finds what appears to be some recently purchased condoms. We both await the punch line. The stillness of our living room. There is no punch line. 'How odd,' I say. What does it mean? Perhaps nothing.

My husband sits still, conveying the pressing immobility of the room via his posture and silence. He goes on beaming his smile at me, less convincingly now. I nudge him. 'I don't know,' I say. 'I don't know either,' he says.

It's true, I might not be as unadulterated as I appear in the company of others, running, being musical. I'm a complicated, a multi-faceted woman. In fact, I don't tell you everything. You should have guessed this by now. And of course, I don't care for vulgarity. But who among us knows a life of spotless purity, pure transparency?

That's what I thought.

�✀ ✀ ✀

It became clear that he wouldn't hear from her during the full week of our spring holiday. Imagine. Not hearing from the one whose every breath you wish to follow. Weekends alone, her silent weekends, demolished him. A week would be too much. An array of thoughts would drive him further into himself at a time when younger people were screwing and demolishing their bodies. It was all an unthinkable burden to him. So two days into the spring holiday would mark the first of his two disappearances.

Where does one go? Where does misery land one? He left no note. *I have to get away, please understand.* No handwritten letter on the kitchen table. *I'll be back.* No. Nothing. He left nothing of the sort.

What is the shape of solitude in a car, on the road—he takes our one car—alone? On the highway driving with your compulsive thoughts, scant attention to the road. Where could he be? Philosophers shouldn't roam alone. A fine hotel with room service, films on television late into the night, a half bottle of liquor that falls to the floor and stains expensive carpet. Or no room service, a destitute environment. A sketchy area off the highway, carpet that feels ill underfoot. The Bates Motel. These things happen.

He showed up two days later, haggard from his wandering. Why did he leave? 'Alone' is all he says at first. Then: 'I had to remember what it's like to exist in a space that isn't populated by others who support or repudiate me.' 'Who repudiate you?' I asked him blankly. He shrugged his shoulders, joined his hands, fingers spread, fingertips touching, as he often does when he's contemplating something grave. But no words followed.

I keep my place on the sofa but don't let him out of my sight. He sits down next to me and takes my hand. Now he's explaining where he's been, what he's seen. Nothing out of the ordinary. 'This was the point,' he says. He wanted to be one more ambiguous object among other objects. People or buildings or forests, road signs, a bed with clean, tightly tucked sheets. 'I did run over and kill an animal,' he says. 'A small animal. It didn't suffer much.' We ponder the significance of this together on the sofa.

On day two of his absence, I was invited to lunch with a trusted colleague, the violinist in my ensemble. We discussed my husband's vanishing, about which I was clearly distraught, but he assured me that all was probably fine. That's the word he chose. All is fine, probably. But I trust him, his musical instincts, so we lunched with as much optimism as we could muster under the circumstances. He's among the most gifted musicians with whom I've had the pleasure to work. He has fine, slender hands. We eventually discussed our upcoming performance, our first in several months. What shall we play, he asked, the Brahms or the Shostakovich? Whatever we like, I said. But even amidst my own turmoil, the thought of having lost my husband, to parasuicide, abduction, and even in the face of a bourgeoning musical radicalism, I secretly longed for Brahms. *Piano Quartet no. 1 in G Minor.*

If I were teaching a course in Literature and Philosophy, the theme would be disappearance. Erasure. How the meaning of words is instantly erased, or canceled, in the wake of said words having been read, spoken, codified, yes. But more importantly, I would focus on the inevitable evacuation of bodies, their ultimate dematerialization in the world of people struggling to interface, to know one another. And yet words and people, sometimes linger, continue to resonate even after they've expired. A mystery to be scrutinized by literature and philosophy, courtesy of Lucille. I'd probably bring music in as well. The fact that composition always has an endpoint.

Notes interact, collide, and then it all comes to a halt. The conclusion is often the most challenging part of a composition to write. The real difficulty: how to finish in such a way that notes are somehow, enigmatically, allowed to reverberate off the page, beyond the score and the fragile, musical gestures made with sensitive hands.

As for the philosopher, the day came when he couldn't write an S. 'It just wouldn't come together,' he tells me later, over dinner. Another pleasant evening on the town, another married couple. 'Ordinarily it wouldn't have been a problem, these are the kinds of things that work themselves out,' he says. Instances of ordinary grace in the otherwise troubled and tempestuous world of the Flesh. But on this day he had the task of writing out a note, an important document, a thank you note to a visiting professor before the latter was escorted to the airport. 'Keep it simple, no need to embellish, but be articulate, no need for humor, just inform our guest of our appreciation in your wonderful way. No one can do it like you,' his department head claimed. Time was essential here, the clock-time of world events. And yet he couldn't get the S down. Attempted corrections made whatever it was – a 5? an incomplete 8? – darker, he kept having to start over. His fingers cramped around the pen. But the letter ended up coming together in the end. These things are generally salvaged with a little effort, though the extra time it took him to write it made him late for a meeting. The head of the department, who esteems him and has an infinite appreciation for his unparalleled contributions and inexplicable talent, was stern and disappointed given the gravity of this particular meeting. After the meeting, Maurice drifted into the corridor and into Terence Prince, an émigré from America and the head custodian in the building that is home to the philosophy department.

Maurice told him his troubles regarding the letter, the tardiness, challenging faculty relations. 'I've seen it all,' said Prince.

As head custodian in such proximity to the philosophy department, he has seen a lot. Arguments, refutations, weeping, obscure laughter, obscene gestures. He's a genuinely decent human being, as my husband put it. 'Everyone trusts him. Prince is our philosophical underbelly, conceptually speaking. He is walking and sweeping pragmatism, and everyone in the department needs him to mitigate our endless theorizing.'

'Our bodies sometimes betray us,' Prince told Maurice that day. He placed his hand on my husband's shoulder. 'We need to take care of them, give them room to fidget, be a little awkward, and then welcome them back with a clean conscience.' Maurice didn't know what this meant but assumed that his motor skills in relation to the cursed letter would eventually return in full. 'As for the meeting,' Prince continued, 'let me talk to the chair on your behalf, one Head to another. We'll smooth this over in no time, you'll see. Incidents always resolve themselves with a bit of patience and compassion. Now go practice your S's.' He let his hand rest on my husband's shoulder for a full seven seconds after delivering this final gift.

Silke. Her hair can be achingly captivating. When it's down it reaches to some unparalleled ideality, some Platonic depth, and it does so without being showy or appearing dolled-up by its owner. One suspects that, even if it's a lie, her hair would feel like her name to the touch. It wouldn't just be any hair. A lucid, sensual comfort to the touch. Or her eyes that stare through you without actually doing that, as a consequence of the shyness that overcomes her, thus making her all the more desirable and penetrating. One yearns to reach her, then, to be familiar enough with her to crack the shell and to feel her enter you with her eyes that are otherwise diverted when the immediacy of two people locked into one another is at stake. The thing that is created between two people as they peer into one another. And what do you see in this unlikely exchange with another whose insight at once paralyzes and inspires you, who compels you to live as you've never lived? What is the shape of your co-creation? It's everything you've ever wanted. It's the structure of form is emptiness, emptiness is form, as the Buddhist says. A woman whose demure exteriority shelters the uncanny capacity to destroy and uplift.

And now, I, too, need to know her, to be pierced by her. One can only admire her distance, it has its charm. But I want more. I want to understand the alchemy that brought her into being and into my husband. What are her specs? And like him, I suspect, I take it personally that she fails to reveal more of herself in the public arena. The Internet is not as powerful as it's often made out to be. As if I, we, are the representatives of all that she wishes to elude. The two of us, alone, though not to the same degree, naturally, his desire and mine. But what is naturally? Why can't I yearn, too? My capacity for desire is faultless, everything's intact there. I want to know the woman who has robbed me of my husband. On a whim, I ran beyond the distance of a marathon yesterday. It was easy, it was nothing to me. But I can't penetrate the veil of another person despite my strong will, my perseverance, the power of technology. I'm starting to resent her obscurity. How convenient it would be to leave it all behind. Like him. And like everybody, in the end. To vanish.

Ten

THE UNIQUE SOUND of an audience prior to taking the stage... We wait in the wings patiently, composed, keeping our nerves in check. The tapestry of indistinguishable voices that will turn into applause and quickly taper off into a respectful stillness as we walk in formation to our respective stations on the stage, and bow in sync. Our black outfits are no surprise; they are elegant. Black is always elegant. Priests, vampires, grieving widows are elegant. On cue, we approach our seats, bow. The instruments have been tuned. All that's left of this ritualistic opening is to sit, assume our positions in relation to strings and wood. A tilted arm, planted feet, a fine, slender hand placed just so. We look at one another, and then to the violinist, and begin.

Shostakovich, *Piano Quintet in G minor, Op.*

57.   Performed with tremendous resolve in the *Chapelle historique du Bon-Pasteur*. My favorite place to perform. With a name like that, how could it not be?

A person in the audience strikes me as singularly attentive in the seconds before we begin. But not to the music. Perhaps I'm merely imagining a solitary admirer in the wake of uncertain relations (my distant husband, you'll recall). But she seems to focus on me alone. I glance at her in moments when my own attention to the score isn't absolutely essential—when I can take in the larger environment, remember myself in a context larger than the music even. She doesn't move to the cadence, her mind is not following the slow gestures, the minute inflections of the composition that envelop us, despite, even, my lapses in attentiveness. No. She's looking solely at me without listening. Improbable in such a space, hearing such music. But I'm a professor of music, I teach and recently published an article on Prokofiev: I generally know when someone is listening or not. She merely follows my movements, hears without listening, my feet on the pedals of the piano. She misses how the instrument dwarfs me in size and yet I rise to meet it with the versatility of my performance. How I play in conversation with skilled others, compliment the light of the room with my own light, sound. She cannot take her eyes off me.

It must have been her. Silke. In retrospect. She knew my occupation. The Internet makes it easy to locate faculty in this era of access (students without publications, substantial vitae, are another story, another vain, epistemological effort). Is she sizing up the enemy? He would have loved this particular construal. Had he been there too, this is the position he would have taken, to be sure. But he wouldn't have known how to handle himself in the presence of us both. He's a philosopher at an impasse. Or perhaps she assumed that the value of her teacher extends to his wife, that she would expand her horizons even further by sharing space with the wife. And why not? Classical music, sure, a beautiful addendum to digital life. But the reality is that he and I are different. I'm valuable in running shoes. At the piano, I channel divinity. But I'm not him; we are not one another. If only I could remember her face and compare it to the woman who appeared at my university office. Who wished to speak to me about my husband. Silke. I was embarrassed to ask her about the performance. Apparently, I don't have his power for love at first sight. To have that face burned into one's memory.

It must have been her. But maybe not. I knew so little then. Now I have a few answers. But hardly enough to warrant peace.

I secretly longed for the Brahms, but the *Quintet* is really a lovely piece, it does everything we need it to do. Notice the bite of the strings, wintry, so common to Shostakovich, that turns into a frolicking quality when the piano directs the movement. The degree to which it takes command! Listen for the piano, what it does in winter, in Russia, or in Montréal, for that matter. And finally, there's the sweeping majesty, the overall sum of Shostakovich. This, even the non-classical music lover must concede. One who merely appreciates a solid soundtrack. There are so many filmic activities one might imagine doing to the Piano *Quintet*. Speeding across central Europe on a train, the uncertainty of the one awaiting you at your destination. Sitting, lying on the floor, thinking intently. This would be the only way to think with the *Quintet* as your accompaniment. I would have preferred the Brahms, but there's nothing like Shostakovich. Familiarize yourself if you haven't already. It'll bring greater depth, more joy to your life. Incidentally, my page turner, whom you may have recognized as being especially keen, yearns to be me. She dresses like me. She wants my identity and life circumstances for her own. If she only knew. But we have a nice relationship. She'll be a fine pianist one day. Perhaps that's what Silke wants, why she may have been there, concentrated. Not to be a pianist, but the independent wife of a noted philosopher. I don't know.

Why keep my musical preference for the night a secret from the others? At this point I'm too tired to make decisions. Weary of the unknown. I'm a feminist in orientation, of course. How can one be otherwise but a force for women? But I've grown exhausted by unknowing. Please, decide for me. Brahms or Shostakovich. Leave or stay, think or don't think. Live or die. Please choose.

He saw her in the distance before class and was suddenly struck by an epiphany. It occurred to him that a subtle but no less authoritative current of under-confidence has always been his companion in relation to women. An entire lifetime of inferiority concentrated in one moment of time. So he froze before her, again, but not in awe. Rather, he assumed that his appearance would be cumbersome to her. This is what he always thought. An intrusion in her day. A leech. A sexual deviant. So he would watch from a comfortable distance, pine for her from the safety of this vantage point, as always. He would martyr his desire. How odd! How inexplicable for someone of his status. What's the soundtrack? Arvo Pärt, *Alina*. Touching music. A moving scene played out on opposite sides of a courtyard. But in the end he opted for a new strategy. He went over to her. And she seemed genuinely happy to meet him. A brief exchange yielded no new insights, just a casual acquaintanceship, two people talking before class, one of whom was in the process of making small but noteworthy leaps.

I had to shop today. My scissors having dug a hole into the bottom corner of my bag—I should have intuited the necessity of covering the blade tips—it's time for a new one. It was old, worn out anyway. Someone such as myself tends to dismiss the value of a good bag. Not anymore. It's an accessory; it too is fashion. Why deny it? Splurge. Treat yourself. At home, both men in my life are happy to see me. One makes no distinction between human limbs and other objects that one might treat as playground equipment. The other lumbers toward me and offers a bite of fruit. We stare at one another without speaking, ingesting pieces of ripe mango. 'You have a new purse,' he says finally.

He's relieved after grading a batch of papers. First, a big stretch off the sofa, a coming back to life. And then cheerfulness: something has lifted. Let's joke around. At his core, Maurice is a goof. He does nothing in particular and I can't control my laughter. He completes his work for the day and does something, makes a noise, a kind of Harpo Marx moment. The cat flees the room in a dash of tail and fur, he—the cat—is genuinely frightened by Harpo Marx, while I grow hysterical and hurt myself laughing. I nearly smack into the dining room table, barely escape broken bones, hospital, stitches. A night in the ER with worn out nurses, arrogant doctors, severely damaged bodies. Running would have been put on hiatus... Then *he* starts laughing. We're here together, sharing a fit that releases hormones and peptides in the body, nurturing good health.

He starts laughing even though in the general arena of the everyday his disappointments have accumulated. They've taken on a life of their own at this stage, constructed a makeshift panopticon at the centre of his being that looks evilly at the proliferating, adolescent cheerfulness. Under its relentless gaze he becomes isolated from others, the rest of us who also know the broken heart. The tender body that can barely stand when affection isn't, or doesn't appear to be reciprocated, can't possibly be returned under the circumstances. He loses perspective on the fact of our mutual fragility. All of us. And how, really, this condition is a fragment of a larger waltz, the suffering we endure. It assumes depth the more we converse with ourselves, with our partners, and listen to them. Listen to what they have to say. Consciousness. I know this because I'm a musician. P. D. Ouspensky on music, laws of being and non-being. My husband, knows this too, but he's forgotten.

Things were warming up. Their exchanges continued. The class plunged deeper into matters of love and death. He began to confide in others. Good for him. I won't name names. Terence Prince. But that's it. A university is a small community. He failed to confide in me, his wife, until it was too late.

But he needed more from her. This is what happens to people in love. He longed for a sign that she also understood the necessity of drifting, of watching the light beneath the window in its summery back and forth. We're in this together, he reasoned in the solitude of his thoughts. In this pastoral miasma of warm, imaginary landscapes. Maurice and Silke. He worked through potentialities, three in total, in the jungle terrain of his thoughts. One: she has absolutely no interest in his affections. Two: she would like to reciprocate his feelings, but feels constrained by her otherwise satisfying partnership. Three: she's far too shy, insecure, in the face of all that he has to offer her, the culture, the ideas, to ever, ever meet him in the space of realized, pounding desire. She knows everything, and is simply afraid of her love. Her jubilant terror in the face of his longing. He clung to this one. His favourite.

His thoughts danced, alone in the figure of a

lost man, on the burnt-out landscape in the wild forests of his imagination. They kept hacking away at perspectives.

There was a fourth possibility: that she had no idea. But this prospect he declined on the basis of her intelligence. She's an adult after all. She reads and reads into the density of texts that relate explicitly or implicitly to the omnivorous demands of relationality, love. She's no fool. Her second short essay was even better than the first. Brilliant. Absolutely first rate.

Eleven

IN THE CLASSROOM, poignancy and insight emerged on the topic of two men in love. He surprised himself, he surprises even me, here, in the way I envision him offering himself to them, to her:

'We reach the novel's conclusion. What does it mean? Any number of meanings. But ultimately, I would argue, what we're dealing with here is tragedy. Again.' He spoke, I imagine, with great care and forcefulness.

'A beloved whose self-contempt precipitates an ongoing struggle to overcome what he perceives as aberrant desire. He struggles through his desire with the aid and authority of tradition, the sheer puissance of that beast. He explores empty, unfulfilling sex with another, a woman, and dreams of his fiancé in another country, yet another prop of a woman. He dreams of a home, a culture far removed from present circumstances that enforces normative sexual codes and thus bears the responsibility of alleviating his desire. Each of these preoccupations collide in him to create aversion to the one person on the planet who receives what a by now familiar philosopher calls the specialty of our desire. We all know what he's talking about. And we know, too, the consequences of not allowing that desire, that person, to direct us, to lead us back to ourselves. This is what desire can do for us. If we let it. And here the lover fails.

But at one point we do find hope in this text. Think back. Another, a swarthy individual whose own ethics of desire are questionable. He offers advice to our protagonist. At once simple and profound. Love him, he says. Here the character echoes the author's general sentiment, summed up nicely in a neat metaphor. Enter the sea. Go under water together, in the space of that marine room, where time is empty. Where you encounter both liberation and sublimation in the other that is the condition of love. A fully confident, conscious, time-depleted, oceanic love.'

His discourse was revving up.

'How might we apply this narrative to our lives today? How might we make the text function for us, as more than a collection of words that presents us with the mathematical task of decoding? What's ultimately at stake here? Do you not see?'

He was ready to pounce.

'Of course. A self, any self that has loved across a boundary. A world traveler, a reader, this is us. Do you hear me? This is us. We are him. Forget sexual orientation for just a moment before making the necessary turn back to his particular predicament. The reality of a vile social construction to which the book clearly speaks, so often a painful, agonizing, violent betrayal of the self, its stupid homophobia, its crass politics.

Let us consider, here in this room, the possibility that we are our own boundaries. Within the limitations prescribed by compassion, conscientiousness, we are free to follow the impulses of the heart. To be less sentimental, the text is inviting us to consider the role of choice in the ever-unfolding trajectories of our lives. Think about this. What are we to do? Philosophy tells us there's a lot to slice through, layers of the social inscribed on the self. I submit that the answer is there nonetheless. Use the text. Let it break and mend you.'

And here he spoke directly to her.

'Love him,' he said.

The irony here was that poignancy and insight, his reaching out to her, to all of them, really, pushed her further away. In the face of her reticence, the under-confidence that may very well be a basement in the general living space of her psyche, his erudition towered, his pedagogy was another world countless light years away. With this intuition following him out of the class, onto the metro, through the door of our home, and plopping down on the sofa with him, or to the floor, a successful class made him nearly as depressed as one in which his audience seemed on the brink of hatred, when the day has been long and everyone is tired.

On a crisp, moderately overcast morning, he carried on a lively forty-two minute conversation with her. Him, alone, running on a gravelly, winding trail. He did most of the talking, naturally. He shared bits of information about his youth, his aspirations, a Fulbright grant at an exceptionally young age. He confided in her about the way he treated a lover many years ago, the ways in which he was treated, what hooked him on philosophy. They ran together across the sylvan terrain of his imagination. But this is not real company. Talking to oneself is neither communication nor self-expression nor love; it's a problem.

She brought up the recent death of a celebrity in an email. Later, when we're together, he thinks to mention it to me. The kind of thing one shares with a spouse when the day's responsibilities have been extinguished, or abandoned. A vacuous comment that still conveys some sliver of importance, our mutual indictment in the steady flow and collapse of existence. But then he decides against it. One of many confessions in his letter to me. In the mental space of his longing, he determines that the celebrity death belongs only to him, to them. I would have been an intruder. It is theirs alone to share.

The parks are repopulated now—not to the extent that they'll be once summer takes full effect of course, but there are bodies roaming. Those with thicker skin sit on a bench for a few moments taking sun.   Young students congregate after school: the afternoon is theirs, anything is possible. I don't need to be that age again, but I do envy the young who have yet to become attached in some modern or traditional variety of wedlock. They experience the lovely ache of people coming and going through their lives as the temporary travelers that they invariably are. Somewhere within, the young understand that everything is transitory and so they are at ease. Occasionally I detour though a park and walk. I enjoy the solitude. There are other lonely park-dwellers here as well, their lives no less significant than my own. It's mostly my own that I weigh in the park, however. And hers. Sometimes I go for hours without even thinking of my husband. She has given me that gift. Someone other than Maurice or myself to contemplate. The music is relatively distant of late. Teaching? I don't know what that is anymore.

'I am nothing more than an afterthought for her,' he tells himself on an especially lousy day. 'I am after thought.' Here he writes with a particularly odd blend of pathos and erudition. An especially pitiable moment in his confession. 'Which is not the same as transcending language, ideas, and operating out of that beautiful spaciousness of no-thought. I have nothing to do with that as far as she's concerned. No. It means that once all thoughts, all consequential ideas, meandering notions even, have been exhausted, in a rare moment of downtime that isn't even sleep, daydreams and other oneiric preoccupations, I might appear to her. A flicker of memory. Barely anything. A misfired neuron, a nothing. Oh, her. And then I fade as quickly as I arose, to be replaced by grander ideas, or, more commonly, routine impressions. I should cut my nails today. The small market on the corner has avocados, two for a dollar. Probably on the verge of expiring. Look, there's the teller at my bank, in the distance, no tie, his hair mussed. My shoelaces won't stop coming undone. I am less than any of these things for her,' he tells me.

Twelve

I'M NOT A MASOCHIST. That's not what this is about. My wishing him well. Wanting him back in my life despite his obsession with another, his disappearance, his unfortunate behavior. So don't jump to conclusions. Don't shake your head. Remember the complexity of life and that a measured quantity of stoicism is useful. That's what gets me through now, even more than the music. It's a stoic interior, regardless of what the exterior does or has to do to get along in the everyday that makes the difference. A considering of the other that gives him what he wants, offers what she needs, while I maintain a solid block of determined placidity on the inside.

And really, masochism has nothing to do with the agony of loss. Unless we're talking about the diminution of physical and sexual boundaries. The relaxing of the coils that keep us so tightly wound. I'm willing to explore these boundaries in physical union. There's power, great pleasure, in submission. And sometimes I enjoy exerting my own dominance. But don't mistake this for disenfranchisement of the self, of the woman. And don't let your imagination go too far. We're just talking about light play here, honest study, laughter between adults in the privacy of their domestic bubble.

But I was surprised to discover, or rediscover, my embarrassment in the bathroom. When I first met him, dated, rented an apartment with him, I was terrified of his hearing the brutal sonic reality of my defecations. I got into the habit of reaching over to the sink—a difficult, intricate process in the architecture of that particular space—and turning on the faucet to mask the sound. This all subsided once we had been together for a year or so, and ended definitively the day he walked into the bathroom, knowing I was there, to search for some cream. My husband and his lotions! This would have been fine, really, we had come to a place of great familiarity with one another. But I was on the toilet, excreting, and, as usual at that point, the faucet was running full throttle. No words were exchanged on the matter. But there I was, sitting still, enveloping the toilet with my legs and ass, and there was the faucet running full on for no apparent reason. I realized a limit was in need of expanding.

And then one day we flash forward and the boundary must once again be erected. Why? The obvious answer is that we're growing apart, in light of things, under the radiant light, the promising touch of Silke. Consequently, I want to keep the undesirable sounds of my body to myself again. Out of a renewed modesty, but also to retain any crumb of sexual appeal I might have to entice him, to keep him with us in our home, where people make noises and create stink, among other things. Now I lock the door. Surely she makes noises too. But he hasn't heard them and probably never will.

No, he remembers her hands from their first brief meeting in his office. Soft, outlined by innocence, somehow indicative of her person. The nails were trimmed, and the palms had a paleness about them that was in no way unhealthy. He must have wondered as I do, to what extent they resembled other parts of her. Places only lovers and doctors venture. He dared not weigh the physical implications of her living with another man, a boy, but restricted himself to visions of her solitary handling of life on the surface of the sea, removed from the aquatic depths into which he desired to plunge with her.

The weeks are flying by with incredible persistence, this is how it always feels as we get older, teaching. The end of the semester is in sight. A double-CD compilation of interpretations and remixes of the music of Erik Satie appears in my campus mailbox. The note says, 'thought you might be interested in this, it's yours to keep, all the best.' I have no interest in sharing the student's name, so don't ask. But it was nice to receive a gift.

There's the story of Satie needing to break up with a woman. For all the splendor and frolicsomeness of his music, he was, it seems, not very courageous in the art of leave-taking. But he was, as one might imagine, exceedingly creative. Rather than tell her face-to-face, 'it's not you it's me, I'm sorry, I'm done,' or even in a note, perfectly (or partly) respectable, he chose to hire a policeman to stand guard at his home. When the woman came round, she was turned away, by the law. It is also known that he collected umbrellas.

Men are not without problems. This includes

the great ones. My husband is great in his own way, in his own atmosphere of living philosophers. Now he's gone.

I lecture on music theory in my classroom, on how it can both enliven and hinder the compositional process. I give them the assignment of composing in a particular mode, a short piece, five minutes tops. Brevity is far more constraining than one would think. Like haiku. Everything has to be perfect, whatever that might mean. We discuss the meaning of successful composition in my course. My student—shall I call him Burlap or Angora? I think not—my student asked more questions than most. I could tell at once that he was genuinely interested in the answers and making every effort to win my attention. It's so simple in class. A raised hand. I'm a teacher, I can recognize these things. Whereas on the outside, there are games to be played, syntactical dances to be performed. And that's if one has a willing partner. Without this, one is quite out of luck.

The student asked questions and spoke to me after class, asked if I had heard this piece or that piece of music—yes, both of them—or what I thought of remix music. We laughed. I'm open, I said. I thought so, he said. The next day I received a double-CD compilation in my campus mailbox. It was lovely to receive a gift. I told him so after our next class.

However, it takes a bold individual to query about the yes or no of a potential coffee when it is in fact shared knowledge of the other's marital status. I wear a ring but not a diamond (Maurice bought me one of these but only after a lengthy discussion of the dangers of ownership, metaphorical imprisonment, etc.). My husband is a philosopher at this very institution. My student asked about the coffee anyway. I said no, but in a manner that was as extended as it was delicate. We left the classroom together. He spoke of ideas for his assignment, we bounced these around, moved them between our fingers. His young, agile hands. He was not an especially promising composer. I wondered, would I have accepted his invitation if he had been? He wasn't bad-looking. But I require a comparable sophistication from a partner, for a date, a coffee. My student took it in stride. He would probably not develop into a significant composer, but he would no doubt meet a woman, marry, and do what those people do when art and ideas have become pastimes and memories.

In the corridor of the music department, not sacred, I was drawn to my own hands. They're like my legs, my feet, all of me, insofar as they're less fleshy than they once were, when I was a teen, or a serious music student in my mid-twenties. They've been worked by the sun, by running. And of course, playing. But they're strong and nimble. It's a treat, I'm told, to watch them undulate upon the piano keys. My first teacher taught me grace of movement. I wouldn't have thought this possible, but it is. They stroke the keys with a buoyancy of touch. They arch, lift, float, strike. What's the soundtrack? Sylvain Chauveau's, *L'approche du Nuage*. Alone, in the corridor, admiring my hands, I debated about wearing mittens in the cold, on my way home.

✂ ✂ ✂

He asked again, the student, after our next class. Coffee. It was becoming tiresome. I'm a tea drinker. I hope you are too. The double-CD was already in a pile of CDs that never gets listened to. He was leaning into me. The situation verged on inappropriate. Though it had been a difficult day. My husband was nowhere to be found. There, before me, in my company, but gone. A mythic creature enslaved by another mythic being whose name has the power to confuse proprioception. So I allowed the student to lean in. His breath was good. He had clearly sucked on a mint before engaging me. I don't know what we looked like together, but I do know that the violinist of my ensemble, who happened to be passing by, stopped and glared. I told the student 'no' again, and sent him to work on his composition. The violinist came over and hissed at me. I didn't have a chance or, really, an inclination to defend myself. You make the decision, I said, and hurried off.

I can't tear myself away from the computer this morning. I'm looking for her again. I discovered where she lives and works. I feel as though I'm beginning to fall asleep. But there's no time for that. Not on a day that's already packed with discoveries. And the sun has not even cast its sheen across the remaining ice.

While walking, in his dazed way of late, from class to the market to pick up some fish—we are not strong meat eaters, I want to be clear, but some fish is healthy, and it's the closest that either of us can get to the sea at this point, winter barely making the curve to spring—Maurice spots yet another woman. She used to serve him tea at a café across from the university. She always smiled and he always looked at her fondly. Positive, resolute, nice style, there was nothing to dislike about her. In fact, he was a little moved by her, he once confessed to me, but always allowed her to pass from his thoughts once his tea was empty and it was time to leave. She wore excellent shoes. But more importantly, he sees her on the way to the market and is unable to forget her for some time insofar as she resembles the one upon whom he has conferred the full breadth of his desire. The barista is softer in her features, taller, slimmer, not quite as angular as Silke. One is sharper in the face, more pitiless than the other. The barista, as it happens, may be younger, but she carries herself, he notices as she crosses the street, with great confidence. He would like to speak to her, ask how she's been, but is too overwhelmed by it all.

He pondered the interchangeability of lovers. Affection-laden objects. What does it say that one's attention can move with such speed from one body to another? From one being and then on to another. He recognized that this common scenario said more about the perceiver than the object of affection. Affection being a fair word here. Love is too strong. But this last assertion is my own wishful thinking. He loved Silke. That's what he claimed, in the end. His love for her covered vast territory, from 'phenomenology to metaphysics'. The occult, even. He brought that in as well. Though I find it inane and would rather not get into it. Perhaps love is simply a matter of intensities. It is always already invoked by virtue of one's infinitesimal existence, paradoxically limitless given the larger cosmic textile of which we are each a woven strand, interwoven with the other, all others. The exclusive claim that one makes on our desire, then, is a bizarre anomaly in the celestial dance. A time-bound ego imperative. And yet there he is. There is Silke, whom he came to love above all others. His love for her so vigilant, so centered to a point of menace that he had to flee. He had nothing more to give, except to her.

Thirteen

SPRING HAS BROKEN. Finally. Some of us have stripped down to nothing more than a medium-weight sweater and jeans, spring shoes. There are few hats now among the masses of springtime amblers in the city. The day is finally upon us when people break out into the streets, smiling, laughing. Even the Hasidic women crack into a laugh once in a while, which they keep to themselves, to their own, though the observant eye of the outsider can catch this moment. I've forgotten how colorful the city can be. This is especially true of our neighborhood. A lovely blend of peoples, talents, children being happy or crying in small parks. There are lively food markets on numerous corners. One, Pakistani owned, has been bombed twice. We're not perfect. And make no mistake. It's still chilly out there.

I'm streamlining. Despite the fact that the semester gets busier as it moves toward the finish line, the running increases for me. When I'm not teaching or preparing for class, I'm running. I'm losing more fat, drying clothes in the dryer to shrink them so that they fit better. Buying new clothes, donating old ones that belonged to another body, one that was able to find contentment in partnership. It ate ice cream when so inclined, sure, why not? The new body barely eats. The old clothes are now in a box somewhere, or being worn by others with their own relational trials, dairy products. I'm stripping it all down to accommodate the needs of a new season. The body, the possessions. Maybe that's what he ultimately does. Streamlines the life. Jettisons the love, the job, the wife, the home, the cat, take it, you can have it all. In the meantime, it's refreshing to pare down. If this is what he's doing, I understand. The burning question: How far will we go?

The dream portion of his letter is a kind of Mallarmé dressed in prose, as he puts it, as all quality dreams are. What's the soundtrack? Debussy, *L'Après-midi d'un Faune*, naturally. The dream followed the oncoming of spring. It's not uncommon for teaching, students, to enter our dreams. If you teach, you know this. So here he is, on a field trip with his students of Literature and Philosophy, hiking through a forest with a winding river as their guide. He's in charge, but moves with anxiety toward their goal, which remains foggy at best. He notes plant life that reminds him of his youth, the small pleasures children take in natural phenomena. Gigantic roots and wild greenery. The fauna, too, scuttle about, dip in and out of perception. The group has splintered into smaller groups, as they do. And eventually he finds himself alone with her, walking on the rugged trail. An easy, parallel stride. The conversation is light, light beaming between leaves and branches in the forest; she speaks openly about herself, who she was in the incarnations of her youth, her likes and dislikes. Their private laughter is friendly, not boisterous. It sounds like the river flowing beside them as they walk, Maurice and Silke following its slow winding current and listening to the quiet babble. Everything is different here. As though the previous months of meandering revelations and unyielding, divisive torment have simply and effortlessly metamorphosed into union. Relief is unfolding for him, finally coming into being. This careful listening, this becoming by her side, rather than at the head of the class, lecturing, a separate being.

The dream takes them through a forest, to a cottage where the hikers and potential lovers eventually stop to rest. The students mill about in and around the cottage; like children, they are not immune to the mysteries of wildlife. Maurice and Silke sit next to one another on a bench in the cottage. The others begin to fade in the light of this pair, their singular glow, everything dims in comparison to them, united at the centre, though this mounting closeness brings luminosity to the entirety of the space as well. Such is the way of French symbolism. And here, in perhaps the most profound moment of tenderness he has ever experienced, in or out of dream life, she moves closer, she pauses, she continues to pause, and then gently places her head on his shoulder. She leans into him, accepts him. He places his arm carefully around her. It is accomplished. Together, they are nature itself. Green energy. The centre of love proliferated, the wise flow of river water.

The others can only notice and approve, frolic, as young people would, in the tributary that engulfs them in watery light. This is where they remain, the illuminated couple. At the centre, at the end of the dream.

What does it mean? Upon awakening, it means that he encountered that split-second division between elation, the unsurpassed power of narrative to send waves of pleasure throughout the body-mind of the dreamer, and then the instantaneous realization that there is no forest, no river, no head on his shoulder, no intimacy with Silke. There is the morning and the unending snake movement of questions, eddies of river water that provide temporary relief, a word from her, and then, always, without fail, abandonment.

What does it mean? She exists first and foremost in his imagination. A living being, to be sure, her body is graceful and strong, her hair is particularly exquisite when reaching for her slim shoulders, she's a fine writer. She stares into one when her courage allows. But for him, her life is in his thought, in waking thought that carries him through a day and determines how he'll behave with others, with her, or with his wife in the morning. Our slow moving into the day with juice, quiet music. What does it mean? In narrative there are prospects.

In my own dream world, I know her, too. I know everything about her. There's nothing in her past or her future that escapes my knowledge. Her body is familiar terrain. The now of her is a fact that I absorb into my consciousness before it even hits the plane of time. And once I arrive at this destination of awareness and expertise of her being, I go against the grain of my general sensibility. I go against music. In the nefarious universe of my sleeping imagination. Listen carefully to what comes next. It's an easy metaphor, clearly, but let's employ it for the potency of its impact. In my dreams I know her, and in the end, I move in on her, in the malevolent forest of my pensive, fabricating mind. I strike with determination for the crime she has perpetrated against my life. With the quick agility of a sprinter, I tear his Silke to shreds.

✂ ✂ ✂

The weekend was nearly over and nothing. No word from her. It was becoming unbearable. He was the last to write and it's only appropriate to expect a response. His constant checking of electronic mail. As though this is some kind of novelty in the very real world of digitized humanity. People who live and speak in abbreviated codes. For him, a philosopher by trade, abbreviation is an act of murder.

Terence Prince was encouraging. He spoke to my husband like a patient father. They stood together just outside Maurice's office, the father coaching his son, letting him know that it'll be okay. Students milling, or rushing around them. 'Yes, I know, I know,' said Terence Prince. 'These things take us apart. They rip curl through our lives, pry us from stability. It can get ugly, violent. Believe me, I know. But you need to hang in there, champ.' I imagine Prince placing a hand on my husband's forearm, leaving it there. 'Give it time. Be compassionate toward all. Including yourself. Know that what you need for fulfillment is right and apparent. In fact, I would go so far as to say that it's already established in the larger scheme of things.' My husband knew what Prince was talking about and felt not a little shame for being so engulfed in misery. However, this knowledge would only take him so far when the gap that was his student pressed in with all of its immense emptiness and suspension. Prince told him to hang in there and proceeded to a meeting with someone in the Fine Arts department. He sauntered down the corridor, sacred, under the observant eyes of my husband, whose self-knowledge is advanced but not without the usual holes and fissures. I wonder who comforts Terence Prince.

Fourteen

SILKE. Perhaps I've been too generous with my fixation. Because really, she's nothing. A girl. A casualty of the times, one more personification of *kitsch*. Look at her outfit here, her posing, what is she thinking? Smart but culturally provincial. Intellectually undernourished. She lacks direction. She reached out to my husband, sought his attention on some ambiguous level, for the advancement of her direction, her girlish satisfaction, who knows, she prompted him beyond the call of duty. How could he not have succumbed to the charm that may or may not have been consciously performed? He can do, he has done, if I can say in all modesty, much better. And really, to hell with modesty. I, a Nobel Prize to her country fair blue ribbon. Prokofiev to her hipster non-music. Clumsy notches of achievement on her bedpost, a rash of boys, dipshits. Before him, I slept with a member of the Bolshoi Opera Company. He's been an incorrigible fool. And she, his anti-muse, is a nothing, a witless adolescent, a dishonest charlatan. She deserves nothing less than the torture of obfuscation her kind inflicts upon the rest of us for whom clarity is the most immediate and obvious of virtues.

The ensemble has collapsed. We all felt it coming. The soundtrack of our demise: Albinoni's *Adagio in G Minor*. With the violinist becoming increasingly derisive in his every comment, no one could do anything right. My own playing being his primary target. This, and then our cellist announces she's moving to Monte Carlo. We don't understand her. How does she do it on such a sparse income? Now it's over. What is music now? Another thing to come undone in the eye of the tempest. I can't think about it now.

The final class is always a mixed bag of sentiment, weariness and the desire to say something profound, to make an indelible impression upon students you will likely never see again, except in dreams. Sometimes this is fine, just fine. It's part of the natural order of things. In other cases, you feel as though something is being lost. A giddy sadness enters your voice as you wish them the very best and send them into summer, a new term, life. It's the same experience for us both. We've discussed this phenomenon at length. For him, with this particular class—you know the one I mean—he knew exactly what he was losing. He opens his bag, pulls out the usual papers, and searches for the right words to encapsulate all that has been said on what became the foremost topics of discussion. His voice—I hear it scuttle across my imagination as though he were speaking this very moment, his tone strong, impacting, emotionally charged. I read the lecture notes on his desk at home:

'The intimacy between love and death is larger than anything broached by our writers. They offer us windows into intimate spaces, private lives. They provide mirrors that reflect back to us our potential, our shortcomings, our minutia of experience, as we navigate love through the body, our immanence, and what we might call, on a positive note, the gift of mortality. A gift because it lends immediacy to the present; it offers a portal of potential insight. What are we doing with our time? How are we endeavoring to overcome time in our lives? These are some of the questions that have directed the trajectory of our course. All handled with more or less delicacy, aesthetic grandeur, subtlety, by the *auteur littéraire et le philosophe*. But these brave men and women can never capture the fullness of our intimate forays into love and its inevitable deathward shift in the life of the individual. This reality is perhaps an underlying tragedy in all literature, in the life of one who attempts but must necessarily fail to communicate the full significance of the event of his or her life. This is where philosophy might have come to the rescue, but of course it too, fails given the limitations of language. Thank you for the effort, Baruch Spinoza.

Recall our tale: A young man wants what he can't have. The object of his love shares his affection, but she's engaged to another. There's no hope of fulfilling his desire. The decision to end his life follows an extensive period of reflection, philosophical contemplation and discussion. And how ironic that he should share this discussion with his beloved's fiancé! As I recall, the class was divided on the value or morality of suicide. For some weakness, for others a legitimate extension of one's humanity in the face of unbearable suffering. But we all agreed with our ill-fated protagonist that neither the sensible nor the healthy have enough influence to sway the suicidalist back to life and well-being.

We do the best we can to survive. We offer what we can to life, we articulate ourselves in the most efficient and thoughtful manner possible. There is love to be had, exhumed from the depths of our many neurotic dramas and dreams, and it will all end, sooner or later, gracefully or otherwise. Or love never blooms. We don't find it, or we fail to muster the courage to accept it as the natural course of life. She escapes us. One way or another, he eschews our restrained advances. Further tragedy. To die without love. To forgo such intimacy.'

✱ ✱ ✱

They spoke that last day. After he raised the mood, became a performer for the last time there, in the room that collapsed in upon the radiant center of Silke. They all laughed. Some felt the sentimental pull of parting. He wished them well and meant it. He made it a point to catch up with her after the last student had gone. He found her walking alone and determined to be by her side for a change, to complement her in the wake of a breezy, temporary farewell prior to their final exam, he went out of his way. Their conversation was comfortable, unforced. It was as though two equals had emerged from a hierarchy, the vestiges of their anxiety dissipating in the synchrony of their steps, a spring day in the city, walking side by side. It was on this day, of course, via this series of collegiate moments shared between them, that his love for her, let's call it what it is, and the tragedy that can sometimes arise from this condition, grew to full maturity. It was the day, we might say in the only slightly melodramatic words of an author, that he knew he was fated to die.

Me? I'm considering a second cat. Another male to inhabit the days that have a mustard feel at this stage. Cheap, yellow mustard, as opposed to the dark German variety. It's the color of my current lenses, figuratively speaking. I know I know this, but removing them is not something I'm very good at these days. I don't even wear sunglasses. I prefer the direct light of the sun, or its cascade across the slick surface of snow, the nearly blinding white. Now I'm being blinded by a sickly yellow, the kind that portends ill health, bad decisions. Substances that one prefers not to see emerging from one's body. The color-producing things one shouldn't do to oneself or to others.

Their walk presaged a deepening of their relations. When all is said and done, this will endure, evolve, he thought. But when Maurice entered that sacred, liminal classroom for the last time to proctor the final exam, the needling question of whether he would ever see her again was a living reality in the thicket of his imagination. How does one do this? Voluntarily cross the threshold into a room that holds the end of their relationship? Even after their walk, after everything. How would he act when she turned her paper in, turned to leave? What would she, either of them say? Oh, but he knew. One thing he knew about Silke was how she would leave him in that room, alone with a group of frenetic examination students paling in importance next to her exit, dramatically understated and thoughtless as it was sure to be. She would say 'thanks' and leave despite the pleasure of their walk. That's how she is. And what could he do? Would he be capable of asserting himself, an anxious child in the body of an esteemed full professor?

But before this moment arrives, imagine the jolt upon entering the room, at seeing her there at the same desk, surrounded by the same faces, but dressed differently than usual, not with the casual attire he found so endearing. She was adorned, in fact, in the apparel of a sophisticated woman. The right scarf, a blouse, a tight-fitting skirt, shoes that preclude running. He paused and took her in. He pushed his imagination over the edge, examined possibilities. She has just stepped out of a terrific European film. She's a painter whose recent show at the Gagosian Gallery won her critical accolades on an international scale. She translates Danish novels when not skiing the Alps. She's a woman whose surface reflects the inner beauty and intelligence that serve as conclusive evidence of goodness and bliss in a world governed by mediocrity. Let's call this outfit what it is: Sexy, sex-infused. But why? Why is she dressed this way? Why is she doing this to him? His thoughts raced toward an impossible finish line. Was he entirely incidental in her world of advanced style, an irrelevant onlooker? He said 'hello', handed out the exam and sat, stunned, afraid of himself.

A brutal passage of time. He heard but did not see her papers rustling. The creaking of her desk alone among all others: a process of attuning himself to her, to her solitary, incomparable light, her blithe, sonic becoming, in the final moments of their time together there. He stole his glances. Her inconceivable sex appeal, those clothes rustling and clawing at his fantasy. And then, suddenly and brutally, the inevitable collaboration of fate and time—the strident unzipping and zipping of her bag for departure. The time would come, he had known it all along, for it to end, this moment of goodbye, of life saying no, the death knell of hope, the blade slicing down and through his neck. He looked up from the book he wasn't reading only as she approached, as though pleasantly surprised. He was right. She left her exam on the desk, said thank you with a quick smile, and turned to leave. Maurice nearly reached out and grabbed her. He did this, in fact, with his voice. He motioned for them to step outside together. The teacher and the student. My husband following his student to the corridor. Others jarred, raised their eyes from their examinations, curious. All coming to a head.

Silke seemed confused. It looked as though his improvisation might go terribly wrong. Even after the nice walk, and all those syncopated steps down the path of their mutual discovery.

In the corridor, he said 'I've enjoyed meeting you.' 'And I, you,' she responded. She looked away. She appeared ill-at-ease in confronting the incomparable stupidity and emptiness of his attempt to prolong the inevitable: the imminence of her walking away, toward the exit door of his life. The door would open and it would close. Gone forever. But he could only stand awkwardly, looking at the floor, taking his gaze out on brief, flitting detours over the terrain of her outfit, and imagine what he would say had liberation been his friend and patron. This was their time. She was killing him. He no longer qualified as a philosopher. He had lost his powers of abstraction. The subjective had taken prominence. He was a dying man.

But he couldn't say these things. He only said goodbye, tried to focus on her eyes as much as possible. There was no handshake, no hug. Perhaps she was so naturally and deeply ensconced in their relationship that these would have been pedestrian to her. But not to him. Give me anything but goodbye. She gave nothing. They parted. He was still, as unbelievable as it may have seemed in that moment, a proctor. How to explain the unexplainable? This is the frantic task of literature and philosophy.

Let's speak briefly about intuition. It knows things that we don't. At once part of us and external to the us that we typically take to be 'I'—all the layers and shifty nuances of self. My husband tapped into this paradoxical otherness and became aware of a definite cloud of inevitability hanging over his thoughts following their parting. He was no longer drifting. The cloud was a dense shadow above and within him that directed his thinking. He felt that she was gone instinctively. He began the grieving process. There in the corridor, a tarnished passage. On Death and Dying. It's finally happened. It was here now. He was at the fraudulent calm of its interiority.

Sometimes intuition is wrong. But he was determined, it seems, to make his own understated exit in the wake of Silke.

His grading in the stillness of our home, quietly focused, following the de-consecration of a room, corridors, all reinvented as negative space. Or not at all focused. It's hard to tell with the way he sat staring at a page, as though entirely absent, only to lift his pen in a sudden motion, let it hover over the page and begin making comments. Her exam, I don't have to tell you, was sheer luminosity, sublime effulgence. Notes for his latest project— love, sex, body, consciousness, performing—were strewn about and again, I didn't know if he was dividing his time between research and grading or merely harnessing time to cultivate what would become his paradoxically subtle jet propulsion out of life. We spoke little in these final days. He blasted through the grading. As always, I helped him organize the software that makes grading efficient and precise. He's terrible at such things. I'm quite good at them.

The last time I saw him was a regular morning, like any other. Nothing unusual. He tells me he has to go into the department for some reason or another, but as it turned out, it was for neither one reason nor another. He never made it to the department. This is when he disappears.

Our last morning consists of a heavier breakfast than usual, and I suppose that's a difference. We speak little. He passes the pepper for the eggs, syrup for the French toast. And at one point he looks at me fondly, a small island of attention, and perhaps gratitude, in an otherwise measureless ocean of distant, morning priorities. The preparing of the food, the eating of the food, moments of staring intently or vacantly, it's hard to tell, in any number of directions. I ponder asking what's gotten into him of late, and this morning in particular, I want to hear him say it—here's your chance on this otherwise lovely morning, spill it, I'll try to understand, we can start over. But the look of serene reverence he gives me prompts me to wait. I'd wait until the evening, until after dinner, I thought. After we've both had an opportunity to run. Maybe I'd suggest that we run together. That would bring us closer, I thought.

And then he leaves. There was no run, no dinner, and no questioning him on his sullen mood. I wait in the afternoon, mildly annoyed by his absence. By evening I was still waiting, concerned. But Montréal, it's a magnificent city, replete with opportunities for fun, adventure, thoughtful diversions. So no problem. He's become preoccupied. By midnight, I know that something has ended. We have ended. Perhaps Maurice's life has ended too—numerous possibilities go through my mind. This disappearance is different from the others, I can feel it. A permanent absence. Thus begins the calling, some crying, galvanizing of faculties, in every sense of that word, and then, of course, finding the letter on his desk. Reading. Into the night. Mesmerized. Convulsions of sadness. The cat by my side. His diving into the sea alone. What could it mean? What did it mean for me?

Fifteen

In my own lucid dreams, I speak to him. For the benefit of my own welfare. I want him to understand that regardless of his predicament, wherever he is, this dramatic turn, this demolishing weight on his life, isn't bereft of value. It's a legitimate, a warranted experience. Even the most shattering events provide us with an opportunity for knowing certain truths, however frail and personal. Remembering what it means to be an activated self amid the sludge of everyday concerns. The self-knowledge of longing and agony. The way he swooned—I know it well for I was once the cause of it. His deep desire speaks to something beautiful. Yes, a stupid, melancholic, calamitous beauty over which I marvel when not engulfed by the ocean of his selfishness. How such forces have worked through him, as they worked through me! But my husband is an exception. An exceptional mind and a sensitive being devoted to beauty and truth. He's always been this way. Self-aware but vulnerable now, to animalisms and baser instincts. On some distant level, on this day in particular, a relatively positive day in the wake of his disappearance, he has my blessing. I want him to be safe. I miss him. I want him back.

Best not to doubt my integrity, nor my feminism and independent spirit, the things my husband used to admire in me. I have too much musicality, too many exacting notes fleshing out my singular existence to forego these qualities. They speak over and against reactionary suspicion. I remain singular, a history, an individual psychology, though I participate in gender and social roles. I'm an astrological sign. I read and compose musical notes according to a Western framework of notation, except when I don't. I live an emotional life. He leaves and I hurt. A parent dies and I'm devastated. The cat gets sick and I'm worried, rushing through traffic to reach the vet before they close. A student makes a move on me and I'm touched. Flattered. Or someone gets angry, becomes vitriolic, I might lash out if you're not careful. Be careful. I feel things. And I'm not afraid to express these feelings. My body aims to colour my mood on occasion. I bleed, this has an effect, though I make efforts to work with the energy of menstruation. I rebel against flowers as a hackneyed sign of affection. But give me a gift, sure, let me know I'm special to you. I rebel against flowery articulation. Heart-speak. But it's my ongoing desire to communicate with clarity and sensitivity. I feel what I say. And I expect one to listen accordingly. My ideas, my experience, music, these are important. My losses are significant. And running. A woman feels the aggregates of her life as fluidity, fluid music, her running, thinking body. And, not without irony, she's sturdy in that movement. She's not just a prop. Woman in motion, aiming to be heard, loved. Sounding her collective voice.

On the other hand, let's not underestimate difference. Between women. Different women.

Take Silke, for example. A woman with her own history, setbacks, the victories of a blossoming intelligence. A strong body. I get the feeling that she has suffered a great deal and come out on top. People like her invariably carry a seriousness within their public personas. I admire her. Perhaps she's the closest I'll ever get to him now.

She knocked on my office door and introduced herself. She'd come to tell me that she was concerned. That makes two of us. But it was genuinely touching, her reaching out like this, her hair was down. She cares, after all, after everything. I noticed the way she sits, a little awkward but self-possessed. She's everything he said she is. Freshly attractive, full of spark, intelligence. But reticent, guarded. But guarded as a mode of being. He had spelled it all out in the letter. I sat listening to her speak of her concern for my husband. And then I told her that he's gone. How much do I say? I said he's gone and I don't know where, or if or when he'll ever return. This was when she almost opened up about him.

About his way of being in the class, with the texts. His good, easy nature. How he sat on a desk and engaged them. Posed a question and waited patiently for an answer. Uncomfortable seconds passing. His halcyon way of being with the students. The details, some focal points of lectures, his preoccupations in class, narratives of his past. The seeming amplification of his passion as he got to know them all, time pressing, each semester streaks by quicker than the last. And eventually, her vague sense that, as the semester wore on, he was speaking directly and exclusively to her. With that passion. Death, love.

I was willing to sit with her for an eternity, and this is no exaggeration. To know her in as much as it's possible to know another. But she eventually excused herself. We both stood. I reached out my hand. I touched her. I even caressed the tip of her finger as our hands came apart in that slow-motion moment of contact that could itself have lasted forever. I sat back down at my desk when she left, abruptly. I contemplated what had just happened. Silke. My tentative conclusion: she's as innocent as a kitten. But we all know how cats can be. Shifty. So this observation does not assuage the fever of loss that comes and goes since the vanishing. If anything, it makes me want to lash out at him. But I can't do this. He's gone. Another outlet then. I have good days and bad. I know where she lives.

Morning meditation. Follow the breath into the abdomen, in and out, up and down. Let this attention grow and extend to the whole body. Seep into that bare attention until it develops even further to include awareness of the observation itself. Become aware of the observer. Rest here. Be present. Be now. Slowly emerge back into clock time having retained something of that paradoxically detached and warmly intimate substratum of the self. Proceed to calm music, tea. In the course of the day, revisit this attention by focusing again on the breath for a minute or so at a time. Or set attention on the limbs. Let it remain on an arm, a leg, the heartbeat, for several seconds. This can be done under any circumstance. At the piano, for instance. But don't perform it, just make it happen. As often as possible.

Guard language. Stand at the gate of what exits the mouth. And more importantly, the thoughts that precede language. What are they? Do they reflect decency and good will?

Be aware of people and their lack of attention. Divide attention between being present to the other and the inner workings of breath, limbs. Intellectual, emotional, or moving points of reference. Notice the same in others. Give them what they need, but remain centralized. Walk against inertia. Run against time.

She lives in a modest home, not far from ours. Silke and her lover, the one to whom, presumably, she divulges her mysteries, her otherwise inscrutable being. A condominium, like most here in the city, in a good neighborhood, in the Mile-End. Now it's me knocking on a door. I wonder if she's home.

A young man opens the door. 'Is this the home of Silke?' I ask. Yes. 'Good, I'm in the right place.' But she's not in. 'Are you her boyfriend?' I ask. Indeed he is. Not what I would have expected, I think. Though the more I stand there and look at him, the more sense it makes. Her being with that body, that haircut, that accommodating, boyish energy standing before me in the doorway of their condo. 'No, no, I'm not exactly a friend,' I say. 'An acquaintance, really, if even that. I've come for her. For either of you.' He doesn't know what to do with this information. He seems anxious, ready for this to be over. Whatever it is.

I hold my ground while I dig through my purse. There's no one around, on this street, at this particular time of day. He watches me, perplexed. My purse is cluttered. I seem a mad person to him. 'How can I help you then?' he asks. 'Just a second,' I say to him, still fumbling, not looking at him, 'there's so much stuff in here.' Time is moving intently, as it does. Like a semester, but much,

much faster here, standing inches apart from her man. And that's fine. It's fine to work only with him. There's a symmetry to it, if you think about it.

I find what I'm looking for at last. It's a big purse. A book bag, really, a relatively new purchase. The young man standing before me, likely younger than she is, has recoiled a few inches. He intuits something wicked. But you know how perplexing intuition can be. I find it, grab hold of it, stand grounded in my active body, attentive to the dynamics of the situation at hand. It's an envelope. Thick. A letter from my husband. Left on his desk before he vanished. Her name, Silke, has been penned in fresh ink, under my own, not so fresh and crossed out. 'Please give this to her. It's hers now. She deserves it.' I stare at him carefully, with the honest intention to mollify. And then I take my leave. Abruptly. Just like she did.

At home, stillness presides, as it does these days. The cat's asleep. He comforts me. Cats are like that. They snuggle into the fold of your neck and this is fine, just fine. This afternoon the cat's asleep. My studio space is immensely still, plant life growing at its glacial pace. Light, through the large windows, is bright without being intrusive. A nice collection of clouds in the sky to dampen the at-times overwhelming sunshine. And to complement my sour mood. Bereaved, lonely, but directed. I'm engaged in this moment, knowing full well its consequences, but eager to lash out, get it over with. I feel as though I have no choice. There's no other way. Love, death. They are so intimately entwined here that even attempting to separate them can be dangerous. I seek only to bring them closer together. This is the moment when I say goodbye to the past.

I reach into my purse, now less cluttered it seems without the letter. It's easier to find what I need now. They reside at the bottom of the bag, a piece of plastic over the tip. I grasp hold of and withdraw the scissors. I remove the plastic. They seem larger now than when I first got them, after I first intuited the need for them. A liberating feeling to wield the scissors. Here they are. No longer stationary or innocuously domestic. Industrial strength scissors. Don't do it, something tells me. But I won't listen to this voice today. I won't. Fuck you, I think in the privacy of my thoughts. They're beginning to surge in and out of control. I don't like it. It's uncomfortable. I'm well beyond the employment of meditation and strategic breathing. Fuck you, I think. I place my thumb and index finger in the slots of the scissors. Hold the pointed tip against my abdomen, where breathing is best observed, where a child would reside for nine months, give or take. As though such grotesque self-annihilation were the answer to my problems. As though this would solve anything. And in one rapid movement I turn the blades outward, tip forward, and attack the piano.

I reach into the body of the piano, the guts, and cut the first, high note wire. It's easy. It snaps in a piercing pop. I pause to consider what I'm doing once more, and then aim for another. The second in line. Pop. Very methodical at first, measured, though I'm beginning to perspire in the light that peaks through clouds and into this space that is rapidly losing its inviolability, its pure musicality. And then I'm indiscriminate, with the midrange wires. Pop, pop, quickly, one after another. The scissors are up for the task. I wasn't sure. And then yet another popping sound, a big snap, issues from inside the abdomen of the piano. A kind of Fluxus or Dada experiment in destruction. Terrible noise and violence. But this is different. A lower, thicker wire cracks as though a whip has been lashed—me, Lucille, I'm the one lashing out—and nearly strikes me in the face. It strikes the outer body of the piano, once immaculate, now cut and bruised. I sense the cat coming to acute, unsettled attention in the other room. Women sense things. I cut another wire. I stand, not grounded. Not musical. Not anymore. Wildly fluid. The last one smacked the lid of the piano, another impossible blemish, a horrifying sound. I beat and cut the body of the piano until my energy gives. I fall on the instrument. I smash it with found objects and start to weep big, gulping tears. We, the piano and I, make abominable music together, deafening reverberations in our once sacred space until I have no more energy for violence and I sense the cat staring at me, his severe concern from underneath the sofa. And then it's done. No more. I stand quietly next to the piano. Me weeping and the other hunched and poised on four legs and uncertain as to his next move. And then? What's the soundtrack? What would make the moment? John Cage, four minutes and thirty-three seconds of relative silence. A classic.

Sixteen

BUT ULTIMATELY, this isn't my tragedy alone. It's also his. A dispatch, written in despair, yes, but in a spirit of awe that trembles at the excesses of human impediment. Dedicated to one who suffers in spite of logic and pragmatist aesthetics and all objective thinking. Yes, in spite of that emotional distance he was once so qualified to administer and to teach… A chance to say what he couldn't or wouldn't say when the glistening object of his thought—for this is primarily what she was, and likely still is for him, a light in his mind that never goes out, or that circles round like the beam of a lighthouse in the dark of night—was quickly fading from physical proximity. Rather than await her slow, murderous disappearance from his life as one awaits certain death in the prison house of insignificance, he determined to dissolve into that night. His epistle, my own letter, another chapter in the frequently uncouth story of literature and philosophy.

With his share of intelligence, ineptitude, he stumbled into love with another woman. In that room, reading her while reading to her there, responding to the subtle enormity of her presence, the splendor of her paradox. The simplest of exchanges with her ignited the fire that melted philosophy and inspired new and better living. He hit an intensity that could no longer live on the margins of mere words. His falling for her less a petty dependence than a willed prostration at her feet.

The violence, the destructive cacophony in an otherwise becalmed home, post-husband, in the wake of Maurice—this is my last distasteful act, no more vulgarity. But it needed to be done. And now, early evening, our home is once again quiet and settled. I feel as though I could become invisible. Like him. But not in that manner, not to life and love, but perhaps to occupation and colleagues. My intention, long nurtured but only recently given a great, heaving impetus, to disappear into a kind of wakeful first condition, a rapture of being—a kind of apocalypse of now where spiritually-rich precautions are one's daily bread, one's every waking moment. Regardless of responsibilities, hissing or deserting others, I'll make the disappearing act my own. I'm a singular woman. I do what's necessary. In the wake of a victimized instrument, I feel there's nothing I can't do. It'll be difficult—being in, but not of the world. Greater musicians than I have tried and failed. But the plan is to evaporate into the loving embrace of my very own unknowing. Sooner or later, we must all slow down, park our reactivity, and come to recognize the value of our suffering. In death, in the paroxysm that can assail love, even pianos.

Finis

Thomas Phillips is a novelist, composer, and teacher known for the minimalist aesthetic that informs his work. In addition to three novels and two collections of horror stories, he has created music for numerous CD releases, installations, and for collaborations in dance and theater. He is also the author of a scholarly monograph on minimalism and has taught in the disciplines of literature and fine arts at various universities in the US, Québec, and Finland.

ALSO OUT THIS SEASON:

THE MATCHSTICK GIRL by Suzanne Hocking
5. 5 x 8.5 | 90 pages | ISBN 978-1-926716-35-0 (pbk.) | $15.88

YELENA walks the line between cold and poverty. Then for a brief moment fortune shines on her and Yelena catches a glimpse of hopes and unknown joys that she never imagined could have been within her reach. But as soon as it appears, it is taken from her. Obsession takes hold, and as the years pass, she grows to want far more than what the life of a young girl of the streets can offer. Through luck and deceit, she lands a place at the esteemed Smolny Institute for Noble Girls where the young women of the Russian court are taught mathematics, literature and science and where Yelena hopes to light a fire under Russian society.

THE MATCHSTICK GIRL brings LGBT undercurrents to nineteenth-century Russia, as our young protagonist struggles with class differences, schoolgirl relationships and her search for self-empowerment.

NOT FOR ART NOR PRAYER by Darren C. Demaree
5. 5 x 8.5 | 90 pages | ISBN 978-1-926716-35-0 (pbk.) | $15.88

Darren C. Demaree's latest collection of poetry.

PRAISE FOR "NOT FOR ART NOR PRAYER"
"...artful and prayerful... ...these generously attentive and marvelously whimsical poems repeatedly resist sleight-of-hand poetic transubstantiation, while slyly acknowledging the inevitably transformative nature of language."
—Lee Ann Roripaugh, Author of Dandarians

"...a crash course in badass alchemy, in concision and razor wire... ...these poems roar through their quiet deftness on the page. Congratulations for picking up this book, you're in for quite a ride."
- Sam Sax, author of sad boy / detective

ARIELLE QUEEN - Book I - A Knight for a Queen by Michel Levesque
5 x 8. 130 pages, ISBN 978-1-926716-32-9 (pbk.) . $13.88

The best-selling, award-winning fantasy series by Michel Levesque translated into English

"Fat. Plain. Orphaned." The three words Arielle uses to describe herself. But a secret, both frightening and beautiful, will emerge, like a butterfly from its cocoon.

BOOK I - A KNIGHT FOR A QUEEN
Arielle, an insecure teenager discovers on her sixteenth birthday that life is not as she once thought—boring. Suddenly thrust into the middle of a battle between evil and more evil that has been raging for centuries she learns of another world co-existing with ours. Now, Arielle must discover who she truly is before she can understand all that is happening around her. A journey of self-discovery becomes a life-and-death struggle for our heroine as she battles supernatural forces pursuing her and learns about herself, her destiny and the prophecies foretelling her arrival.

TO RUSSIA WITH LOVE by Damian Siqueiros

To Russia with Love" is how a group of Montreal artists and collaborators answer the phobias arising out of Russia. This is their stand against the recent wave of bigotry and violence and the realization of the moral imperative to not remain passive in the face of hatred and injustice.

"...exquisitely detailed...." - Phil Tarney, Artists Corner Gallery, Hollywood, California

"Masterful visual quotations.." - Ivan Savvine, Russian Journalist & Activist

Led by visual artist and photographer Damian Siqueiros, "To Russia with Love" portrays iconic gay and lesbian Russians in all of Siqueiros's usual detail and flare. Along with his collaborators, Mr. Siqueiros is passionate in his belief that fighting hatred with hatred is as nonsensical as trying to extinguish a fire with more fire. There is no condemnation for those perpetrating injustice, instead these portraits serve to remind us of the beauty of love and to validate the couples and the identities of our Russian brothers and sisters in the LGBT community.

A Selection of other 8th House Titles

SEVEN SYRIANS - War Accounts from Syrian Refugees by Diego Cupolo

8 x 8. | 86 pages | Full-Color Photography | ISBN 978-1-926716-26-8 | $18.88

"Seven Syrians" captures the stories and struggles of those caught in the middle of the armed conflict currently ravaging Syria. Framed by Diego Cupolo's unerring eye while touring the region, these photographs and first-hand accounts remind us that it is civilians who suffer the brunt of war's atrocities. In a series of humanizing portraits, Diego Cupolo takes us into the lives of those fortunate enough to have survived the conflict decimating their homeland. Forced to flee their homes and families, these men, women and children, teachers, plumbers, engineers, taxi drivers, brothers and sisters no different than ourselves and our neighbours, tell us in their own words of their struggles, triumphs, pains and fortitude and of the monstrosity of war when all of us the world over, seek the same security and opportunities for our children. Read and listen.

THE ENGLISH QABALAH 2nd. Edition, Hardcover

7 x 9.25 | 440 pages | Hard Cover | ISBN 978-1-926716-26-8 | $56.00

A learned exposition by one of the world's leading Qabalists, this book takes the reader through an exploratory journey through the English Alphabet and the mystic and even subconscious roots of our development of language throughout history. A quick survey of the Hebrew Qabalah is presented before embarking the reader upon the discovery of the English Qabalah and the Key to the Roman Script published here for the first time. Disturbingly poetic and irritatingly profound, readers will find a treasure chest of delights to whet their curiosity. - Editor's Review

THE MIDAS TOUCH BY James Cummins & Cameron W. Reed

230 pages. ISBN 978-1-926716-06-0 $23.88

" .. a journey into the predatory nature of some of the practices and institutions in the financial industry today ."

Authors James Cummins and Cameron W. Reed take us on an exploratory journey into the predatory nature of some of the practices and institutions in the financial industry today. What seems innocently enough as capitalism and greed gone naturally wild in an environment of deregulation, soon appears as deliberate political manoeuvering and close control on an international scale by agents and institutions operating above the law.

CROSSING TO TADOUSSAC by Frederick E. Bryson
438 pages, 5 x 8, ISBN 978-1-926716-00-8

The FLQ have bombed the Montreal Stock Exchange. The streets are charged and a referendum is called on secession. Frederick E. Bryson captures a defining moment in Canadian history in his latest novel "Crossing to Tadoussac".

KOLKATA DREAMS by K. Gandhar Chakravarty
Colour, Illustrated. ISBN 978-0-9809108-7-2

A work that will transport you across the sea to the idealization and mysticism of the East against the realities of its westernization. Reading and reciting this poetry, you will find that laughter often chokes itself on tears while the book yo-yos between meditation and contemplation.
"A robust, deceptive simplicity hums at the center of this collection..." - YUSEF KOMUNYAKAA, PULITZER PRIZE WINNER FOR POETRY ON "KOLKATA DREAMS"

JUMP THE DEVIL by Richard Rathwell
5 x 8. 146 pages, ISBN 978-1-926716-11-4. $18.88

With Jump the Devil, Richard Rathwell has masterfully interwoven the plots of five seemingly unrelated storylines to create one coherent narrative that spans the globe and works to blend the seemingly mundane with the profound, deftly providing readers the necessary clues to unlocking the story. Transcending borders, cultures, generations, and social mores, Jump the Devil brings to life the notion of the global village as it exists in the 21st Century.
Rathwell's writing is "a fistful of sentences written with the subtlety of a geisha and the terse certainty of stainless steel." - JOHN OLSON, AUTHOR

HYPODROME by Jason Price Everett
148 pages, 5 x 8 ISBN: 978-1-926716-12-1

Jason Price Everett's poetry explodes from the page with the raucous power of industrial machinery and strikes its targets with the rapier's fine point. Honing in on the chaos of the past two decades, Hypodrome charts the growth of today's artist searching for the defining aesthetic of our time. These poems document the plastic, the losses, the frustrations and the triumphs accumulated during the course of an accelerated era set against the backdrop of an ominously beautiful future.

UNFICTIONS by Jason Price Everett
288 pages, 5 x 8. ISBN 978-0-9809108-6-5

Unfictions serves to dramatize the way in which we react to such an information-rich environment in all of its glorious simultaneity - the beginning of a type of 'New Realism' in letters - reflecting faithfully a society so saturated with events and quotations that it can no longer distinguish between them and their relative meanings. "

"...a remarkable achievement and issues a profound challenge to the literary landscape of today." - THE ANTIGONISH REVIEW ON "UNFICTIONS"

MAVOR'S BONES BY ROLLI (CHARLES ANDERSON)
5 x 8 | 121 pages. ISBN 978-1-926716-30-5 (pbk.) | $15.88

"I have been dreaming / those dreams of meaning / that come from the waters / of dreaming deep / like drowned men / to the gold skin / of the ocean"
Company's come. In a ramshackle mansion, meet a family in the same condition—ancient, decayed. There's the brooding Duke, and his riotous brother. There's Grandam, lost in wilds of herself. There's a vicar, a philosopher, an angel, a ghost or two. And somewhere above them all, in a ruined garret...
"By turns delightfully black, singingly lyrical and/or innocently nonsensical. Here is a poet outside the mainstream with his own refreshingly original voice and bone[s] to pick." – Gillian Harding-Russell, author of I Forgot to Tell You

Visit us online at www.8thHousePublishing.com

www.ingramcontent.com/pod-product-compliance
Lightning Source LLC
Chambersburg PA
CBHW031333060726
47590CB00007B/2440